Alfred Tennyson

Guinevere

Alfred Tennyson

Guinevere

ISBN/EAN: 9783337418199

Printed in Europe, USA, Canada, Australia, Japan

Cover: Foto ©Andreas Hilbeck / pixelio.de

More available books at **www.hansebooks.com**

TENNYSON

GUINEVERE

WITH

INTRODUCTION AND NOTES

BY

G. C. MACAULAY, M.A.

FORMERLY FELLOW OF TRINITY COLLEGE, CAMBRIDGE

London

MACMILLAN AND CO.

AND NEW YORK

1895

PREFACE.

THIS edition of *Guinevere* is uniform with that of *The Coming of Arthur* and *The Passing of Arthur*, by Mr. F. J. Rowe of the Presidency College, Calcutta, and with my own editions of *Gareth and Lynette, The Marriage of Geraint, Geraint and Enid*, and *The Holy Grail*. For a general account of Tennyson's poetry, and especially of the *Idylls of the King*, I may be permitted to refer to Mr. Rowe's Introductions.

It is difficult for any except practical teachers to realise how much help is needed by young students in order that they may understand and appreciate what they read in English literature, and often the more apparently simple a passage is, the more it needs a note, in order that its full meaning may not be missed. This must be my apology for having explained in the notes many things which may be thought to be already sufficiently obvious. I have found myself, and my own experience has been confirmed by others, that there is hardly anything which school-boys of fair intelligence are not capable of misunderstanding, and I have gradually, and rather unwillingly, become convinced, that it is better to make the notes too many than too few. Especially it is desirable, with a view to those who are reading only a

single idyll, that frequent references should be given to
the others of the same series, in order to make their con-
tinuity more evident, and that parallel passages should be
quoted from Tennyson generally, to illustrate points of
style and the usage of words.   In the introduction I have
endeavoured to make clear the general plan of the *Idylls
of the King* and the relation of *Guinevere* to the rest,
while at the same time I have quoted enough of Malory's
Morte Darthur to enable the reader to understand something of Tennyson's manner of dealing with the sources
from which his stories are drawn.   Etymologies of words
have been noted where they seemed to supply illustration
of their meaning, and for this I have used Dr. Skeat's
Etymological Dictionary.   For the quotations from Malory
I have used the Globe edition of the *Morte Darthur* with
modernised spelling, as more intelligible to youthful
readers.   Other obligations are acknowledged as they
occur.

CONTENTS.

INTRODUCTION.

THE idyll of *Guinevere* was published first in 1859 as one of that group of four studies of female character from the Arthurian cycle, which first had the title *Idylls of the King.* These were *Enid, Vivien, Elaine,* and *Guinevere,* and of them the last alone has remained without change of title. After an interval of ten years in 1869 appeared another volume, *The Holy Grail and Other Poems,* including *The Coming of Arthur, The Holy Grail, Pelleas and Ettare,* and *The Passing of Arthur,* the last being the *Morte d'Arthur* published in 1842, with some additions; in 1871 *The Last Tournament,* in 1872 *Gareth and Lynette,* and finally in 1885 *Balin and Balan* were added, and the whole was arranged in a series of twelve idylls (*Enid* being divided into two), in which *The Coming of Arthur* serves as introduction and *The Passing of Arthur* as conclusion, while the remaining ten have as a general title *The Round Table.*

I.

Before the appearance of the volume containing the *Holy Grail,* in 1869, it was impossible to form a conception of the work as a whole. The four idylls which first appeared seemed to be, and perhaps were, simply four independent delineations of woman's character, representing in the person of Enid the ideal of maidenhood and wifehood, in Vivien the type of falseness and impurity, in Elaine that of impulsive and wilful , girlhood, and in Guinevere that of the erring and repentant wife. It was not, therefore, until the publication of the next volume that the structure and moral drift of the work began to be perceived, and afterwards the addition of *Gareth and Lynette* as the first, and of *The Last Tournament* as the last of the Round Table series, made the artistic effect far more complete. In fact, notwithstanding the early indica-tions in the introduction to the fragment called *Morte d'Arthur*, that an Epic upon the subject had formed one of the young poet's designs, it is probable that the work as we have it at present only gradually took shape in his mind, and that its unity is not the result of a fully preconceived plan. Indeed, the very title *Idylls of the King* seems to indicate that the first design was of a series of picturesque narrative poems each one complete in itself, and however happily it may express the leading characteristic of the poet's style, would hardly have been adopted for a fully worked out Epic of King Arthur. Many, indeed, who perceive this and who learnt first to admire and love the idylls before they had a distinctly visible plan, are disposed even now to deny that the series can profitably be regarded as a single poem, while others are unable to conceive of the completed work having grown in the manner which has been suggested without a design definitely formed from the first, and are disposed to regard the poet as having planned his Epic in fulness from the days when the *Morte d'Arthur* was written, and to have worked it out gradually with full consciousness of the final aim throughout. One indeed, a German, suggests that the author, knowing his public, was well aware that a whole Epic at once was too much for its digestion, and therefore dealt out to it fragments from time to time until the whole was put forth. He cannot otherwise account for the moral and artistic unity which he finds in the completed work. It is more probable that this unity, which unquestionably exists, is due to the fact that the separate poems of which it is composed, besides being the work of a single mind with very definitely formed artistic aims and moral ideals, were welded together by the author in the years which followed the first publication with a design, which did not at first exist, of presenting them as a single work having something of the form of an Arthurian Epic.

However this may be, the intention of the author that the *Idylls of the King* should be regarded as an artistic whole is made quite clear in the address to the Queen which concludes the work, and in which he has indicated its unity and moral purpose :

"Accept this old imperfect tale,
New-old, and shadowing sense at war with soul,
Rather than that gray King, whose name, a ghost,
Streams like a cloud, man-shaped, from mountain peak,
And cleaves to cairn and cromlech still ; or him
Of Geoffrey's book, or him of Malleor's, one
Touch'd by the adulterous finger of a time
That hover'd between war and wantonness,
And crownings and dethronements."

We are not therefore to look in the *Idylls* for a historical presentation of the Celtic Arthur, nor yet for a reproduction of the hero of mediæval chivalry, such as we find him in Geoffrey of Monmouth's *Historia Britonum*, or in Malory's *Morte Darthur* : the framework of the old romances is used, but the tale is modern; and to find fault with the poet for making his heroes think the thoughts and speak the language of the nineteenth century would be as little reasonable as to find fault with the authors of the romances of *Merlin* and *Lancelot* for making their personages, whom they imagine to have lived in the fifth century, think and speak like men and women of the thirteenth and fourteenth. Tennyson himself has warned us what to expect from him in this way,

"Why take the style of those heroic times?
For nature brings not back the Mastodon,
Nor we those times."[1]

And we must not therefore be surprised to find in the *Idylls of the King*

"King Arthur, like a modern gentleman
Of stateliest port,"

or that, far from regarding the modern touches as anachronisms to be avoided, he looks upon them as the essential feature of the work—that which redeems it from the charge of nothingness which might attach to the mere remodelling of models.

The tale then, as completed, has a definite moral aim. It is not an allegory, for the characters are men and women, not personified qualities; but it has a spiritual

[1] *The Epic*, 35.

meaning, it shadows "Sense at war with Soul." It is true that the spiritual meaning was far less obvious in the first four idylls than in those which followed them, and that the highly developed symbolism of *The Holy Grail* and *Gareth and Lynette* is in marked contrast with the simplicity of narrative which we find in *Enid* and *Elaine*. But though the methods of treatment are different, all unite to produce a single moral effect. Arthur represents the spiritual force that works to make the dead world live, which for a time has power to accomplish its purpose, but is gradually overborne and goes down. The strife, however, is one which is ever to be renewed; Arthur is deeply wounded, but he cannot die; he passes to the mystic island valley to heal him of his wound, and he will one day come again and finish the work which he has begun. The hero has been victorious over the external foe, he has conquered rebels and heathen invaders; his failure is due to a more subtle enemy, to the taint of moral corruption which creeps in among the circle which he has gathered round him

> " To serve as model for the mighty world,
> And be the fair beginning of a time."

He is betrayed, and the purpose of his life is spoilt by those whom he most trusted to join with one will in his work and make it perfect:

> " And all whereon I lean'd in wife and friend
> Is traitor to my peace, and all my realm
> Reels back into the beast, and is no more."

Yet it would be a mistake to regard the spirit of the poem as pessimistic. The German critic to whom we have already referred can see nothing of hope in Arthur's failure. "A great and noble hero has for a time succeeded in working out his ideal of man in . . . the souls of his fellow-beings; there is a moment when all the knights of the Round Table bear the likeness of the king. But the moment passes. The resistance of matter, of the flesh, grows stronger every day, until at last every spark of ideal life is quenched in the body of Arthur's knighthood; another illustration of Goethe's famous words,

> 'Dem Herrlichsten, was auch der Geist empfangen,
> Drängt immer fremd und fremder Stoff sich an,' etc.

A glorious world disappears in the rising flood of sin and wickedness, and nothing remains but a blank. We look into an empty future. In this pessimistic view of life Tennyson shows himself a child of his time : how different is this end from that planned by Spenser for his *Faerie Queene*, which was to end with the realization of the perfect ideal through the marriage of Arthur and Gloriana," etc. ! [1]

If it be pessimism to have recognised that the problems of life are far more complex than men have thought, and that the perfect ideal is not so easily realised, even by the marriage of Arthur and Gloriana, as the sixteenth century, to which nothing seemed impossible, was apt to believe, then Tennyson is a pessimist. In any other sense the name is totally inapplicable. According to his teaching the individual may be defeated of his full purpose, but his work does not perish ; he represents a force which cannot die, and if this or that

[1] Hamann, *Essay on Tennyson's Idylls of the King.*

purpose of men seems to have failed, yet God will fulfil himself none the less in other ways of which we dream not. The individual man must be content to say with Arthur,

> "I have lived my life, and that which I have done
> May He within Himself make pure!"

Of the twelve idylls of which the whole poem now consists *Guinevere* stands last but one, and contains in fact the tragic catastrophe of which the actual Morte d'Arthur, the subject of the concluding idyll, is only the necessary complement.

In *The Coming of Arthur* we see the king established on the throne, wedded to Guinevere, and victorious over Rome and the heathen.

In *Gareth and Lynette* there is set before us the spring-time of Arthur's glory, when the Round Table seemed to be indeed "a model for the mighty world," and the king himself the representative of Christ upon earth. No sensual taint has yet crept in, or at least none is visible; it is the period referred to afterwards as the time

> 'When every morning brought a noble chance,
> And every chance brought out a noble knight."

In the symbolical war of Time against the soul of man, the soul is here decisively the victor.

The two succeeding idylls, *The Marriage of Geraint* and *Geraint and Enid*, are in fact one, in spite of the division. In subject they lie a little apart from the general scheme of the *Idylls*, but they contribute to it some essential elements. They show us the first insidious approach of corruption, the beginning of the moral taint which is soon to become apparent. It would not be possible, without violent shock, to pass directly from *Gareth and Lynette* to *Merlin and Vivien*; but the suspicions of Geraint prepare us for "the world's low whisper breaking into storm," which we so soon afterwards hear; and at the same time Enid, as a type of pure and loyal wifehood, serves as a contrast to Guinevere.

Balin and Balan was added as an introduction to *Merlin and Vivien*, and in these two idylls we realise how far the evil has spread. The tragedy of the two brothers is directly due to loss of faith in Guinevere's purity; and Merlin with all his varied powers falls a prey to the seductions of Vivien. The victory of sense over soul seems to grow more and more assured.

In *Lancelot and Elaine* some of the fruits are harvested of the seed which has been sown. Elaine's maiden love for Lancelot is set against the Queen's guilty passion; and so closely intertwined is that which is noble and knightly in Lancelot with his sin, that honour and dishonour, the true and the false, are no longer distinguishable. Elaine's life is wrecked; and Lancelot breaking out into bitter remorse, is yet unable to burst the bonds which defame him.

All other means of redemption having failed, there remains only that which is offered by religion. In the *Holy Grail* we reach, as it were, the critical point. The members of this society, worst and best alike, are seized by an impulse of enthusiasm, and vow themselves to the pursuit of an object which can only be attained by purity. And what is the result? The best indeed succeed, but their aims are thereby turned wholly away from this earth, and the Round Table sees them no more. Their service in the work of cleansing the world is lost, and the influence of their purity ceases to leaven the society of which they were members. Of those to whom the vision came, one cares only to pass into the silent life of prayer, "leaving human wrongs to right themselves," and another is seen no more in this world, however he may be crowned king in the spiritual world. Of the rest, the worst are made more reckless in their sin ; and though some in whom a noble nature has been dragged down into the mire, but not so as to have the eyes of the soul utterly blinded with clay, struggle desperately to raise themselves, yet when the enthusiasm is over, and they find themselves left in a society which has been deprived of its purest elements and seems condemned to a fatal degeneration, they almost inevitably return to their former path.

In *Pelleas and Ettarre* we see something of the younger generation of knights who have come in to fill the gaps left by the Quest of the Sangrail. The disillusion of Pelleas, who has come to the court so full of youthful faith in chivalry and loyal love, is a new evidence of the prevailing corruption. The Queen cowers before him, raw youth as he is, because she feels that now indeed her secret is known, while Modred mutters to himself that the time is hard at hand.

The Last Tournament reveals a startling picture of moral anarchy. Arthur himself cannot help perceiving the degeneracy, slow as he has been to suspect any evil. The obedience of the knights is less loyal, and their bearing less noble than before; the kingdom threatens to "reel back into the beast." A mock Round Table has been founded elsewhere in scorn of the vows taken and broken by Arthur's knights, and while Arthur is quelling what he conceives to be the last stand of the powers of evil, the prize in the Tournament of the Dead Innocence, over which he leaves Lancelot to preside, is won by Tristram, the most frankly sensual of Arthur's knights, the worldling of the world, who almost openly scoffs at his vows, and who carries off the ruby necklace as an offering to Isolt. When Arthur returns, "all in a death-dumb autumn-dripping gloom," he finds the bower of the Queen dark and all the work of his life destroyed.

The Queen has fled to the convent of Almesbury, having refused to accompany Lancelot to his own land; and there in the idyll of *Guinevere* we find her, not having told her name, but received and sheltered by the peaceful Sisterhood because of her grace and beauty and the power of persuasion which she has. She knows that she has done ill and that terrible ruin has come of it; but as yet she cannot lighten her soul by shrift and hardly even by tears. She can only listen to the heedless talk of the little novice who is her constant companion, and repeat the burden, "Too late, too late!" which she had moaned to herself as she fled. The little maid, by her thoughtless prattle, hurts where she would heal, and is driven away by a sudden storm of anger from the Queen; who then reflecting on her guilt, goes back to the golden days when first she knew Lancelot, and becomes half-guilty in her thoughts again, notwithstanding her repentance. On a sudden a cry through the house announces the King, who returns from waging war with Lancelot to deal a blow at the treason which has declared itself in his absence. He has learnt at length where the Queen has taken refuge, and he comes to take a last farewell of her in this world, and to set before her the wrong which she has done to himself and to the land. Yet though he will never see her again, and though he may not even touch her lips or take her hand, he cannot but love her still, and he solemnly charges her to purify her soul, that so they may meet again "in that world where all are pure," and she may claim him as her husband. Then in the darkness he bends low over her prostrate form, and waves his hand in blessing above her head. He departs, and she has been unable to utter a word of farewell. She staggers to the casement, and sees him sitting on horseback at the door, giving charge to the nuns, who stand near with torches, to guard and to foster her; but his helm is lowered, and she cannot see his face. He turns and moves away through the moonlight mist, seeming like the phantom of a giant in it, and becoming grayer and more ghostlike as the vapour enwinds him fold by fold. Then at last she finds a voice, and cries after him passionately,

"Gone—my lord !
Gone thro' my sin to slay and to be slain !"

But she remembers the hope which he has held out to her, and resolves to meet him, if she may, in that purer life, and to tell him there that she loves him and no smaller soul,

"Not Lancelot nor another."

And so, received as a sister by the nuns, she wears out the close of her life in almsdeed and prayer, and at length passes away to her rest.

Such is the outline of this noble poem, in which the human and dramatic interest rises to a higher pitch than in any other of the idylls. As to the high level of poetry and of eloquence which is here attained, there can hardly be two opinions, but there is probably an under-current of feeling in the mind of most readers which prevents the poem from having exactly the effect which the poet intended. We cannot help feeling that the fault lay not wholly with her, a woman made to love and to be loved, but partly also with the man who chose her for his helpmate, supposing that she would think his thoughts and share his purposes, and took no pains to win her love or to guard her from temptation. We cannot admit the right of this husband to cast all the blame upon his wife, and then to forgive her "as Eternal God forgives." We feel that there is something to be said for her which the poet has not said.

It is interesting from this point of view to compare Tennyson's idyll with the poem by William Morris (published in 1858, the year before the first publication of the *Idylls of the King*) called *The Defence of Guenevere*; and it is worth noting incidentally how much the attention of English poets must have been turned at that time to the Arthur romance. Guenevere, accused by Gawaine, makes a defence before her judges, and says :

"Suppose your time were come to die,
And you were quite alone and very weak,
Yea, laid a-dying, while very mightily

" The wind was ruffling up the narrow streak
   Of river through your broad lands running well :
   Suppose a hush should come, then someone speak :

" 'One of these cloths is heaven, and one is hell,
   Now choose one cloth for ever ; which they be
   I will not tell you, you must somehow tell

" ' Of your own strength and mightiness : here, see.'

  . . . .

" And one of these strange choosing cloths was blue,
   Wavy and long, and one cut short and red ;
   No man could tell the better of the two.

" After a shivering half-hour you said,
   'God help ! heaven's colour, the blue,' and he said ' hell !'
   Perhaps you then would roll upon your bed,

" And cry to all good men that loved you well,
   ' Ah Christ ! if only I had known, known, known !'

  . . . .

" Nevertheless you, O Sir Gawaine, lie,
   Whatever may have happened through these years ;
   God knows I speak truth saying that you lie."

Then after relating how Lancelot came to the court
and of her long months of misery,

" Behold, my judges, then the cloths were brought.
   While I was dizzied thus, old thoughts would crowd,

" Belonging to the time ere I was bought
   By Arthur's great name and his little love :
   Must I give up for ever then, I thought,

" That which I deemed would ever round me move
   Glorifying all things ; for a little word,
   Scarce ever meant at all, must I remain

" Stone-cold for ever ?"

Something, no doubt, there is to be said from this point of view, but it is true nevertheless that those who choose wrong in matters of the highest import are inexorably punished, and that the sin which is committed in high places and brings with it the ruin of a kingdom must be denounced with greater sternness than ordinary sins. There will always be those in whose estimation grace and beauty are a sufficient palliation for almost any offence, but it is well to be reminded that they are not everything, and that they who fail to see and to love the highest must expiate their failure by suffering. On the whole, the criticism which must be admitted is rather that the Arthur of the *Idylls* is too impersonal really to attract our sympathies, and that we are therefore almost as incapable as Guinevere of appreciating

"That pure severity of perfect light."

This defect, however, is perhaps inseparable from the symbolical character of the work. It was impossible that the representative of Soul in its conflict with Sense should have much of the human weakness which attracts and endears. After all, we must remember that the young poet's epic, "King Arthur," is supposed to have been thrown into the fire, in order that something more modern might be substituted for those "faint Homeric echoes," and all that we have left of it is contained in the last of the idylls, where we do really succeed in getting nearer to the person of the hero, and begin to find out that he is a human creature after all.

II.

It is needless to say that we shall find in *Guinevere* the same characteristics of style which we have already noted in the other idylls. The most important of these are a wonderful richness of picturesque description and imagery combined with extreme simplicity of diction, and in the versification an almost perfect command of all the harmonies of language and of the effects which may be produced by the rhythmical combination of sounds. In the matter of picturesque description and simile Tennyson may fairly be said to stand first among English poets. He sees with unsurpassable accuracy and with the eye of an artist, and is able to sum up for us that which he has seen in phrases which have all the effect of a revelation—the characteristic which he himself has attributed to Virgil, of producing magical effects by single words and phrases. Examples of this picturesqueness will readily occur to the reader of Guinevere, but the deeper dramatic interest of the situation and the high tone of serious eloquence which characterises the speech of the king naturally render this particular quality less prominent here than in some of the preceding idylls. The best examples are contained in the description of the signs and wonders which filled the land before the coming of the Queen (ll. 230-268), where we have the fine picture of the headlands down the coast of Lyonnesse,

> "Each with a beacon star upon his head,
> And with a wild sea-light about his feet,
> He saw them—headland after headland flame
> Far on into the rich heart of the west,"

and immediately succeeding it the delicately beautiful description of the flickering fairy-circle which wheeled and broke before the horse of the traveller at evening, and the wreath of airy dancers which swung round the lantern of the hall. Still more imaginative is the picture of the bard chanting his mystic lay on the cloud-covered mountain-tops,

> " When round him bent the spirits of the hills
> With all their dewy hair blown back like flame."

Then again we recall the picture of Lancelot and Guinevere riding

> "under groves that look'd a paradise
> Of blossom, over sheets of hyacinth
> That seem'd the heavens upbreaking thro' the earth,"

or of the king on horseback at the door in the moonlight mist, through which blazed the golden dragon on his helmet, reflecting the light of the torches and making all the night a steam of fire. Of similes it may suffice to mention the very pretty one of the three gray linnets wrangling for the thistle seed (l. 252 ff.), and that of the stream which spouting from a cliff disperses itself in spray as it falls, but gathers again into a stream at the base,

> "Remakes itself and flashes down the vale"

(604 ff). Yet this richness of workmanship is combined, as has been said, with a singular simplicity of materials; and it is this combination which more than anything else makes the poet's style individual. The simplicity of Tennyson's diction is closely connected with his preference for words which belong to the original Eng-

lish stock over those imported from French or other languages. The proportion of purely English words in his verse is perhaps larger than in the works of any great English poet since Chaucer ; and though many of those words in the English language which are of foreign origin are as popular as those of native stock, yet at the same time, since the less popular element in the language is mostly of foreign origin, a diction which is almost wholly English can hardly fail to be simple and popular. A reviewer of the four idylls which were published in 1859, remarks that "since the definite formation of the English language no poetry has been written with so small an admixture of Latin as the *Idylls of the King*, and what will sound still stranger in the ears of those who have been in the habit of regarding the Latin element as essential to the dignity of poetry, no language has surpassed in epic dignity the English of these poems."[1]

This characteristic is nowhere more remarkable than in *Guinevere*, where Arthur's pathetic eloquence finds expression in the very simplest words, and lines which often consist entirely of monosyllables have a tragic dignity which is not surpassed by Milton,

> "And all thro' thee! so that this life of mine
> I guard as God's high gift from scathe and wrong,
> Not greatly care to lose ; but rather think
> How sad it were for Arthur, should he live,
> To sit once more within his lonely hall,
> And miss the wonted number of my knights,
> And miss to hear high talk of noble deeds
> As in the golden days before thy sin,"

[1] *Edin. Rev.* 1859.

or again,

> " Yet not less, O Guinevere,
> For I was ever virgin save for thee,
> My love thro' flesh hath wrought into my life
> So far that my doom is, I love thee still.
> Let no man dream but that I love thee still,
> And so thou lean on our fair father Christ,
> Hereafter in that world where all are pure
> We two may meet before high God, and thou
> Wilt spring to me, and claim me thine, and know
> I am thine husband—not a smaller soul,
> Nor Lancelot nor another. Leave me that
> I charge thee, my last hope. Now must I hence."

No finer effect has ever been produced by means so simple.

In regard to the versification of the poem it is not necessary perhaps to analyse minutely the various elements of rhythmical harmony which contribute to the whole effect. The poet is master of his instrument of expression, as a great musician is master of his pipes or strings, and produces the effects which he requires without much separate attention to the technical elements on which they depend. The use of alliteration, the harmonious and discordant collocation of sounds, or the imitation in the rhythm of the action described are matters probably of unconscious habit, and ought not to be represented by the critic as so many artifices, each used separately by the poet to produce a given result. If we desired to imitate the effect, no doubt, it would be necessary to study closely the means by which it is produced, but for the appreciation of a beautiful passage it is not the best way to begin by this kind of analysis.

Enough that the poet is master of the delicate instrument upon which he plays. For most writers the liberty acquired by discarding "the troublesome and modern bondage of riming" proves to be rather dangerous, but for such a poet as Tennyson it could not be anything but a gain to exchange so formal a method of satisfying the ear for the free exercise of his own sense of harmony. In his hands blank verse is not only a beautiful and dignified form of expression for the ordinary narrative, but also a most flexible instrument for representing emotion and action by rhythm. It has very great variety in accent, pause, and cadence, and the trochaic or dactylic rhythm is freely alternated with the iambic, often producing the happiest effect. Take for instance such a passage as the following:

> " A murmuring whisper thro' the nunnery ran,
> Then on a sudden a cry, 'The King.' She sat
> Stiff-stricken, listening; but when armed feet
> Thro' the long gallery from the outer doors
> Rang coming, prone from off her seat she fell,
> And grovell'd with her face against the floor:
> There with her milk-white arms and shadowy hair
> She made her face a darkness from the King:
> And in the darkness heard his armed feet
> Pause by her; then came silence, then a voice,
> Monotonous and hollow like a Ghost's
> Denouncing judgment, but tho' changed, the King's."

In contrast with this variety we often find an intentional monotony, designed to give additional effect to that repetition of word or phrase which is so often employed by the poet either for emphasis or pathos, as,

"It was my duty to have loved the highest :
It surely was my profit had I known :
It would have been my pleasure had I seen."

But the examination of particular passages with reference to their rhythmical qualities will find a place more
properly in the notes. It is enough to say here that
there is hardly any variety of rhythmical effect of
which Tennyson's blank verse is not capable.

III.

The source of the story, so far as Tennyson has
followed any authority, is to be found in Malory's
Morte Darthur. He has not followed this authority by
any means closely, but it has suggested most of the
leading features in the story, and it will therefore be
necessary to quote from it at some length, in order
that we may make clear both the poet's obligations to
his predecessors and also his originality.

The twentieth book of the *Morte Darthur* thus begins,
—I quote from Sir Edward Strachey's ("Globe") edition
with modernised spelling :—

"In May, when every lusty heart flourisheth and
burgeneth ; for as the season is lusty to behold and
comfortable, so man and woman rejoice and gladden
of summer coming with his fresh flowers : for winter,
with his rough winds and blasts, causeth a lusty man
and woman to cower and sit fast by the fire ; so in
this season, as in the month of May, it befell a great
anger and unhap that stinted not till the flower of
chivalry of all the world was destroyed and slain : and
all was long upon two unhappy knights, the which

were named Sir Agravaine and Sir Mordred, that were brethren unto Sir Gawaine. For this Sir Agravaine and Sir Mordred had ever a privy hate unto the queen dame Guenever, and to Sir Launcelot, and daily and nightly they ever watched upon Sir Launcelot. So it mis-happed Sir Gawaine and all his brethren were in king Arthur's chamber, and then Sir Agravaine said thus openly, and not in no counsel, that many knights might hear it : I marvel that we all be not ashamed both to see and to know how Sir Launcelot goeth with the queen, and all we know it so, and it is shamefully suffered of us all, that we all should suffer so noble a king as king Arthur is, so to be shamed. Then spake Sir Gawaine and said, Brother, Sir Agravaine, I pray you and charge you, move no such matters no more afore me ; for wit ye well, said Sir Gawaine, I will not be of your counsel. Truly, said Sir Gaheris and Sir Gareth, we will not be knowing, brother Agravaine, of your deeds. Then will I, said Sir Mordred. I believe well that, said Sir Gawaine, for ever unto all unhappiness, brother Sir Mordred, thereto will ye grant, and I would that you left all this and made you not so busy, for I know, said Sir Gawaine, what will fall of it. Fall of it what fall may, said Sir Agravaine, I will disclose it to the king. Not by my counsel, said Sir Gawaine, for and there rise war and wrake betwixt Sir Launcelot and us, wit you well, brother, there will many kings and great lords hold with Sir Launcelot."[1]

Gawaine reminds his brothers of the kindnesses they have received from Sir Launcelot; and finally

[1] Bk. 20, chap. 1

when the king comes in, and Agravaine and Mordred are about to tell him of the matter, Gawaine, Gaheris, and Gareth go out with sorrow at their heart, feeling that now the noble fellowship of the Round Table shall be dispersed. Agravaine then tells Arthur, who is loth to move in the matter without positive proof. He authorises Agravaine and Mordred to lie in wait for Launcelot and take him, if possible, in the queen's chamber. So on the morn Arthur rides out hunting, and sends word to the queen that he will be out all night ; and Agravaine and Mordred take twelve knights to watch with them for Launcelot's going to the queen. Launcelot, though warned of the danger by Bors, insists on going to speak with the queen.

" So Sir Launcelot departed and took his sword under his arm, and so in his mantle that noble knight put himself in great jeopardy, and so he passed till he came to the queen's chamber. And then, as the French book saith, there came Sir Agravaine and Sir Mordred, with twelve knights with them of the Round Table, and they said with a crying voice, Traitor knight, Sir Launcelot du Lake, now art thou taken. And thus they cried with a loud voice, that all the court might hear it : and they all fourteen were armed at all points as they should fight in a battle. Alas, said Queen Guenever, now are we mischieved both. Madam, said Sir Launcelot, is there here any armour within your chamber, that I might cover my poor body withal, and if there be any, give it me, and I shall soon stint their malice. Truly, said the queen, I have none armour, shield, sword nor spear, wherefore I dread me sore our long love is come to a mis-

chievous end; for I hear by their noise there be many
noble knights, and well I wot they be surely armed,
against them ye may make no resistance; wherefore ye
are likely to be slain, and then shall I be burnt. For,
and ye might escape them, said the queen, I would
not doubt but that ye would rescue me in what danger
that ever I stood in. Alas, said Sir Launcelot, in all my
life was I never bested that I should be thus shamefully slain for lack of mine armour. But ever in one
Sir Agravaine and Sir Mordred cried, Traitor knight,
come out of the queen's chamber, for wit thou well
thou art so beset that thou shalt not escape. O
mercy, said Sir Launcelot, this shameful cry and noise
I may not suffer, far better were death at once than
thus to endure this pain. Then he took the queen
in his arms and kissed her, and said, Most noble
Christian queen, I beseech you, as ye have ever been
my special good lady, and I at all times your true
poor knight unto my power, and as I never failed
you in right nor in wrong since the first day that
king Arthur made me knight, that ye will pray for
my soul if that I here be slain. For well I am
assured that Sir Bors my nephew and all the remnant
of my kin, with Sir Lavaine and Sir Urre, that they
will not fail to rescue you from the fire, and therefore, mine own lady, recomfort yourself whatsoever
come of me, that ye go with Sir Bors my nephew
and Sir Urre, and they all will do you all the pleasure
that they can or may, that ye shall live like a queen
upon my lands. Nay, Launcelot, said the queen, wit
thou well I will never live after thy days, but and
thou be slain, I will take my death as meekly for

Jesu Christ's sake as ever did any Christian queen.
Well, madam, said Launcelot, sith it is so that the
day is come that our love must depart, wit you well
I shall sell my life as dear as I may, and a thousand
fold, said Sir Launcelot, I am more heavier for you
than for myself. And now I had lever than to be
lord of all Christendom, that I had sure armour upon
me, that men might speak of my deeds or ever I
were slain. Truly, said the queen, I would, and it
might please God, that they would take me and slay
me, and suffer you to escape. That shall never be,
said Sir Launcelot, God defend me from such a
shame; but, Jesu, be thou my shield and mine
armour."[1]

The knights attempt to batter down the door,
which Launcelot unbars and holds open a little, so
that one man could come in. There came in Sir
Colgrevance, and Launcelot slew him and armed himself in his armour, with the help of the queen and
her ladies. Then he strode out among them and
slew Sir Agravaine and the twelve knights and wounded
Sir Mordred, who fled.

"And then Sir Launcelot returned again unto the
queen and said, Madam, now wit you well all our true
love is brought to an end, for now will king Arthur
ever be my foe, and therefore, madam, and it like
you that I may have you with me, I shall save you
from all manner adventures dangerous. That is not
best, said the queen, me seemeth now ye have done
so much harm, it will be best ye hold you still with
this. And if ye see that as to-morn they will put

---

[1] Bk. 20, chap. 3.

me unto the death, then may ye rescue me as ye think best. I will well, said Sir Launcelot, for have ye no doubt, while I am living I shall rescue you. And then he kissed her, and either gave other a ring, and so there he left the queen and went until his lodging."[1]

Launcelot comes to Bors and tells him of his adventure, and gathers together his friends to counsel. They agree that if the queen is condemned to the fire, Launcelot shall rescue her. Meanwhile Mordred carries news to king Arthur, who is grieved to think that the noble fellowship of the Round Table is now broken up, and forthwith the queen was condemned to the fire, in spite of the pleading of Gawaine in her favour. It is ordered that on the morrow the queen shall have her judgment and receive her death; but Gawaine refuses to be present, and Gaheris and Gareth, being commanded to be there, will only come unarmed.

"And then the queen was led forth without Carlisle, and there she was despoiled into her smock. And so then her ghostly father was brought to her, to be shriven of her misdeeds. Then was there weeping and wailing and wringing of hands, of many lords and ladies. But there were few in comparison that would bear any armour for to strength the death of the queen. Then was there one that Sir Launcelot had sent unto that place for to espy what time the queen should go unto her death. And anon, as he saw the queen despoiled into her smock and so shriven, then he gave Sir Launcelot warning. Then was there but spurring and plucking up of horses, and right so

[1] Bk. 20, chap. 4.

they came to the fire, and who that stood against them, there they were slain, there might none withstand Sir Launcelot, so all that bare arms and withstood them, there were they slain—full many a noble knight. . . . And so in this rushing and hurtling, as Sir Launcelot thrang here and there, it mishapped him to slay Gaheris and Sir Gareth the noble knight, for they were unarmed and unaware, for as the French book saith, Sir Launcelot smote Sir Gareth and Sir Gaheris upon the brain pans, where-through they were slain in the field : howbeit in very truth Sir Launcelot saw them not, and so were they found dead among the thickest of the press. Then when Sir Launcelot had thus done, and slain and put to flight all that would withstand him, then he rode straight unto dame Guenever, and made a kirtle and a gown to be cast upon her, and then he made her to be set behind him and prayed her to be of good cheer. Wit you well the queen was glad that she was escaped from the death, and then she thanked God and Sir Launcelot. And so he rode his way with the queen, as the French book saith, unto Joyous Gard, and there he kept her as a noble knight should do, and many great lords and some kings sent Sir Launcelot many good knights, and many noble knights drew unto Sir Launcelot."[1]

The king was deeply grieved at the rescue of the queen and the death of his knights, "much more I am sorrier for my good knights' loss than for the loss of my fair queen, for queens I might have enow, but such a fellowship of good knights shall never be together

[1] Bk. 20, chap. 8.

in no company." Gawaine, who has hitherto taken the part of Launcelot, is exasperated against him by the news of his brother's death, and urges Arthur to make war upon him. Accordingly, the king and Gawaine lay siege to the castle of Joyous Gard, but Launcelot keeps himself within and will not bear arms against the king who made him knight. At the same time he offers to make it good against any other that Guenever is a true lady to her lord. At length, moved by the taunts of Gawaine, he comes out to battle, and his side has somewhat the better, though Launcelot himself has no heart to fight against the king. Meanwhile the Pope, having heard of this quarrel, sends down bulls to make peace, bidding Launcelot to deliver up Guenever and the king to accord with Launcelot. Accordingly, Launcelot delivers up the queen under condition that she shall suffer no punishment, and he again offers to make it good against all comers, excepting Arthur himself, that she is a true lady to the king. Gawaine, however, will not suffer the king to agree with Launcelot, and the latter, after in vain endeavouring to make his peace with Gawaine for the death of his brothers, sorrowfully leaves the realm and passes over sea. The king and Gawaine prepare a great host to go after him, and they lay siege to the city of Benwick, while Mordred remains as governor of England and guardian of the queen. Then Mordred caused news to be brought that Arthur was slain, and he made the lords choose him king and prepared to marry queen Guenever. She, however, escaped from him to the tower of London and defended herself against him there, while

Arthur, hearing of the events in England, raised the
siege of Benwick and hastily returned.   Mordred met
him at Dover and endeavoured to prevent his landing,
but was defeated.   On the king's side, however,
Gawaine was slain.   Again Mordred was defeated upon
Barham Down, and finally retired westward to the
neighbourhood of Salisbury.   Here, on the Monday
after Trinity Sunday, the battle was fought in which
Mordred was slain and Arthur wounded to the death.
"Yet some men yet say in many parts of England
that king Arthur is not dead, but had by the will of
our Lord Jesu in another place.   And men say that
he shall come again, and he shall win the holy cross.
I will not say it shall be so, but rather I will say
that here in this world he changed his life . . . .
And when queen Guenever understood that king Arthur
was slain, and all the noble knights, Sir Mordred and
all the remnant, then the queen stole away, and five
ladies with her, and so she went to Almesbury, and
there she let make herself a nun, and wore white
clothes and black, and great penance she took, as ever
did sinful lady in this land, and never creature could
make her merry, but lived in fasting, prayers and
alms-deeds, that all manner of people marvelled how
virtuously she was changed.   Now leave we queen
Guenever in Almesbury a nun in white clothes and
black, and there she was abbess and ruler, as reason
would ; and turn we from her and speak we of Sir
Launcelot du Lake."[1]

Of the rest of the story, how Launcelot came to
England and found Guenever at Almesbury, and how

[1] Bk. 21, chap. 7.

he vowed to forsake the world, as she had done, and took the religious habit in a hermitage, and how Guenever died and was buried by Launcelot in the tomb of Arthur at Glastonbury, and how soon after this Launcelot himself died and was buried,—of these things no more need here be said, because Tennyson has passed them over without mention.

This then is the story, as it is told by Malory, following his French book, and it is obvious at once how far different both in general tone and in incident from that which is presented to us by Tennyson. In the *Morte Darthur* we find a state of society in which the only practical test of loyalty and chastity is the trial by combat, and in which the lady whose champion is victorious is not only freed from the penalties of her unfaithfulness, but is regarded as completely cleared of reproach. Arthur orders Guenever to be burnt "in his heat," but it is more for causing the death of his knights than for any other reason; and Launcelot delivers her up to him at last with a certificate of fidelity founded simply on the fact that no one dares to challenge his assertion by combat. The war with Launcelot is almost wholly grounded upon the desire to avenge the death of Gawaine's brethren, and the catastrophe depends only in a very remote degree upon Guenever. Launcelot and she are models of what lovers should be, and the idea of remorse does not enter into their minds so long as all goes well. The death of Arthur is the event which drives Guenever into a nunnery, for though a wife may have lovers, it is hardly so decent for a widow; and Launcelot's fidelity to her leads him to adopt the same kind of life, not-

withstanding that she urges him to take a wife in
his own country. Evidently this kind of story, with
its incidental barbarity of wife-burning, is not suitable
as it stands for the poet's purpose. It may be more
epic, and perhaps also more dramatic, than that which
he has adopted, but it will not do for "Sense at
war with Soul." Everyone must admire the delicacy
and skill with which Tennyson, while retaining most
of the incidents of the old story, has adapted it to
his purpose. He has given us a Guinevere who is
already suffering tortures of remorse and apprehension,
and a Lancelot who is willing to part from her at her
entreaty. The sympathies of the modern reader are
still further moved in her favour by her refusal to
accept Lancelot's offer of a refuge at Joyous Gard,
but at the same time they are not caused to revolt
against Arthur by any barbarous sentence of death.
If any such was passed in the first heat, it was
speedily revoked. The whole interest is concentrated
upon the moral issue: it is the sin of Guinevere
which brings about the whole catastrophe; and whereas
in the romance the repentance comes, if it comes at
all, after Arthur's death; while the interview at
Almesbury is not between Guinevere and Arthur, but
between Guinevere and Lancelot; we have here a
true penitent lying at the feet of a husband whose
life she has ruined, and by the omission of the later
incidents the poet has avoided that division of interest
between Arthur and Lancelot which to a great extent destroys the unity of the romance. Indeed
the true hero of the latter part of Malory's *Morte
Darthur* is rather Lancelot than Arthur, and it is

with the death of Lancelot that the conclusion is made. There is no doubt that the Arthur of the *Idylls*, shadowy though his personality may be, is a more worthy hero than the Arthur of the romances, and that the Guinevere of the *Idylls* is a person in whom we feel the deepest human interest. There will always be persons who feel outraged because the motives of the mediæval romances have been altered and the characters remodelled, persons who would rather see Guinevere burnt than preached to ; but it is difficult to deny the claim of the poet to re-write the old stories in accordance with the moral ideals of his own age, and this claim is made with the utmost distinctness, both in the lines which accompanied the first publication of his *Morte d'Arthur*, and in those already quoted from the address *To the Queen* at the conclusion of the *Idylls*.

GUINEVERE.

Queen Guinevere had fled the court, and sat
There in the holy house at Almesbury
Weeping, none with her save a little maid,
A novice : one low light betwixt them burn'd
Blurr'd by the creeping mist, for all abroad,
Beneath a moon unseen albeit at full,
The white mist, like a face-cloth to the face,
Clung to the dead earth, and the land was still.

For hither had she fled, her cause of flight
Sir Modred ; he that like a subtle beast   10
Lay couchant with his eyes upon the throne,
Ready to spring, waiting a chance : for this
He chill'd the popular praises of the King
With silent smiles of slow disparagement ;
And tamper'd with the Lords of the White Horse,
Heathen, the brood by Hengist left ; and sought
To make disruption in the Table Round
Of Arthur, and to splinter it into feuds
Serving his traitorous end ; and all his aims
Were sharpen'd by strong hate for Lancelot.   20

For thus it chanced one morn when all the court,
Green-suited, but with plumes that mock'd the may,

S   A

Had been, their wont, a-maying and return'd,
That Modred still in green, all ear and eye,
Climb'd to the high top of the garden-wall
To spy some secret scandal if he might,
And saw the Queen who sat betwixt her best
Enid, and lissome Vivien, of her court
The wiliest and the worst; and more than this
He saw not, for Sir Lancelot passing by   30
Spied where he couch'd, and as the gardener's hand
Picks from the colewort a green caterpillar,
So from the high wall and the flowering grove
Of grasses Lancelot pluck'd him by the heel,
And cast him as a worm upon the way;
But when he knew the Prince tho' marr'd with dust,
He, reverencing king's blood in a bad man,
Made such excuses as he might, and these
Full knightly without scorn; for in those days
No knight of Arthur's noblest dealt in scorn;   40
But, if a man were halt or hunch'd, in him
By those whom God had made full-limb'd and tall,
Scorn was allow'd as part of his defect,
And he was answer'd softly by the King
And all his Table. So Sir Lancelot holp
To raise the Prince, who rising twice or thrice
Full sharply smote his knees, and smiled, and went:
But, ever after, the small violence done
Rankled in him and ruffled all his heart,
As the sharp wind that ruffles all day long   50
A little bitter pool about a stone
On the bare coast.

           But when Sir Lancelot told
This matter to the Queen, at first she laugh'd
Lightly, to think of Modred's dusty fall,
Then shudder'd, as the village wife who cries
'I shudder, some one steps across my grave;'

Then laugh'd again, but faintlier, for indeed
She half-foresaw that he, the subtle beast,
Would track her guilt until he found, and hers
Would be for evermore a name of scorn.   60
Henceforward rarely could she front in hall,
Or elsewhere, Modred's narrow foxy face,
Heart-hiding smile, and gray persistent eye :
Henceforward too, the Powers that tend the soul,
To help it from the death that cannot die,
And save it even in extremes, began
To vex and plague her. Many a time for hours,
Beside the placid breathings of the King,
In the dead night, grim faces came and went
Before her, or a vague spiritual fear—   70
Like to some doubtful noise of creaking doors,
Heard by the watcher in a haunted house,
That keeps the rust of murder on the walls—
Held her awake : or if she slept, she dream'd
An awful dream ; for then she seem'd to stand
On some vast plain before a setting sun,
And from the sun there swiftly made at her
A ghastly something, and its shadow flew
Before it, till it touch'd her, and she turn'd—
When lo ! her own, that broadening from her feet,
And blackening, swallow'd all the land, and in it 81
Far cities burnt, and with a cry she woke.
And all this trouble did not pass but grew ;
Till ev'n the clear face of the guileless King,
And trustful courtesies of household life,
Became her bane ; and at the last she said,
'O Lancelot, get thee hence to thine own land,
For if thou tarry we shall meet again,
And if we meet again, some evil chance
Will make the smouldering scandal break and blaze
Before the people, and our lord the King.'   91
And Lancelot ever promised, but remain'd,

And still they met and met. Again she said,
'O Lancelot, if thou love me get thee hence.'
And then they were agreed upon a night
(When the good King should not be there) to meet
And part for ever. Vivien, lurking, heard.
She told Sir Modred. Passion-pale they met
And greeted. Hands in hands, and eye to eye,
Low on the border of her couch they sat   100
Stammering and staring. It was their last hour,
A madness of farewells. And Modred brought
His creatures to the basement of the tower
For testimony; and crying with full voice
'Traitor, come out, ye are trapt at last,' aroused
Lancelot, who rushing outward lionlike
Leapt on him, and hurl'd him headlong, and he fell
Stunn'd, and his creatures took and bare him off,
And all was still: then she, 'The end is come,
And I am shamed for ever.;' and he said   110
'Mine be the shame; mine was the sin: but rise,
And fly to my strong castle overseas:
There will I hide thee, till my life shall end,
There hold thee with my life against the world.'
She answer'd, 'Lancelot, wilt thou hold me so?
Nay, friend, for we have taken our farewells.
Would God that thou couldst hide me from myself!
Mine is the shame, for I was wife, and thou
Unwedded: yet rise now, and let us fly,
For I will draw me into sanctuary,   120
And bide my doom.' So Lancelot got her horse,
Set her thereon, and mounted on his own,
And then they rode to the divided way,
There kiss'd, and parted weeping: for he past,
Love-loyal to the least wish of the Queen,
Back to his land; but she to Almesbury
Fled all night long by glimmering waste and weald,
And heard the Spirits of the waste and weald

Moan as she fled, or thought she heard them moan :
And in herself she moan'd 'Too late, too late !'   130
Till in the cold wind that foreruns the morn,
A blot in heaven, the Raven, flying high,
Croak'd, and she thought, 'He spies a field of death ;
For now the Heathen of the Northern Sea,.
Lured by the crimes and frailties of the court,.
Begin to slay the folk, and spoil the land.'

And when she came to Almesbury she spake
There to the nuns, and said, 'Mine enemies
Pursue me, but, O peaceful Sisterhood,
Receive, and yield me sanctuary, nor ask   140
Her name to whom ye yield it, till her time
To tell you :' and her beauty, grace and power,
Wrought as a charm upon them, and they spared
To ask it.

                    So the stately Queen abode
For many a week, unknown, among the nuns ;
Nor with them mix'd, nor told her name, nor sought,
Wrapt in her grief, for housel or for shrift,
But communed only with the little maid,
Who pleased her with a babbling heedlessness
Which often lured her from herself ; but now,   150
This night, a rumour wildly blown about
Came, that Sir Modred had usurp'd the realm,
And leagued him with the heathen, while the King
Was waging war on Lancelot : then she thought,
'With what a hate the people and the King
Must hate me,' and bow'd down upon her hands
Silent, until the little maid, who brook'd
No silence, brake it, uttering 'Late ! so late !
What hour, I wonder, now ?' and when she drew
No answer, by and by began to hum   160
An air the nuns had taught her ; 'Late, so late !'

Which when she heard, the Queen looked up, and said,
'O maiden, if indeed ye list to sing,
Sing, and unbind my heart that I may weep.'
Whereat full willingly sang the little maid.

'Late, late, so late! and dark the night and chill!
Late, late, so late! but we can enter still.
Too late, too late! ye cannot enter now.

'No light had we: for that we do repent;
And learning this, the bridegroom will relent.   170
Too late, too late! ye cannot enter now..

'No light: so late! and dark and chill the night!
O let us in, that we may find the light!
Too late, too late: ye cannot enter now.

'Have we not heard the bridegroom is so sweet?
O let us in, tho' late, to kiss his feet!
No, no, too late! ye cannot enter now.'

So sang the novice, while full passionately,
Her head upon her hands, remembering
Her thought when first she came, wept the sad Queen.
Then said the little novice prattling to her,   181

'O pray you, noble lady, weep no more;
But let my words, the words of one so small,
Who knowing nothing knows but to obey,
And if I do not there is penance given—
Comfort your sorrows; for they do not flow
From evil done; right sure am I of that,
Who see your tender grace and stateliness.
But weigh your sorrows with our lord the King's,
And weighing find them less; for gone is he   190
To wage grim war against Sir Lancelot there,

Round that strong castle where he holds the Queen ;
And Modred whom he left in charge of all,
The traitor—Ah sweet lady, the King's grief
For his own self, and his own Queen, and realm,
Must needs be thrice as great as any of ours.
For me, I thank the saints, I am not great.
For if there ever come a grief to me
I cry my cry in silence, and have done.
None knows it, and my tears have brought me good :
But even were the griefs of little ones   201
As great as those of great ones, yet this grief
Is added to the griefs the great must bear,
That howsoever much they may desire
Silence, they cannot weep behind a cloud :
As even here they talk at Almesbury
About the good King and his wicked Queen,
And were I such a King with such a Queen,
Well might I wish to veil her wickedness,
But were I such a King, it could not be.'   210

Then to her own sad heart mutter'd the Queen,
'Will the child kill me with her innocent talk ?'
But openly she answer'd, 'Must not I,
If this false traitor have displaced his lord,
Grieve with the common grief of all the realm ?'

'Yea,' said the maid, 'this is all woman's grief,
That *she* is woman, whose disloyal life
Hath wrought confusion in the Table Round
Which good King Arthur founded, years ago,
With signs and miracles and wonders, there   220
At Camelot, ere the coming of the Queen.'

Then thought the Queen within herself again,
'Will the child kill me with her foolish prate ?'
But openly she spake and said to her,

'O little maid, shut in by nunnery walls,
What canst thou know of Kings and Tables Round,
Or what of signs and wonders, but the signs
And simple miracles of thy nunnery?'

To whom the little novice garrulously,
'Yea, but I know: the land was full of signs   230
And wonders ere the coming of the Queen.
So said my father, and himself was knight
Of the great Table—at the founding of it;
And rode thereto from Lyonnesse, and he said
That as he rode, an hour or maybe twain
After the sunset, down the coast, he heard:
Strange music, and he paused, and turning—there,
All down the lonely coast of Lyonnesse,
Each with a beacon-star upon his head,
And with a wild sea-light about his feet,   240
He saw them—headland after headland flame
Far on into the rich heart of the west:
And in the light the white mermaiden swam,
And strong man-breasted things stood from the sea,
And sent a deep sea-voice thro' all the land,
To which the little elves of chasm and cleft
Made answer, sounding like a distant horn.
So said my father—yea, and furthermore,
Next morning, while he past the dim-lit woods,
Himself beheld three spirits mad with joy   250
Come dashing down on a tall wayside flower,
That shook beneath them, as the thistle shakes
When three gray linnets wrangle for the seed:
And still at evenings on before his horse
The flickering fairy-circle wheel'd and broke
Flying, and link'd again, and wheel'd and broke
Flying, for all the land was full of life.
And when at last he came to Camelot,
A wreath of airy dancers hand-in-hand

Swung round the lighted lantern of the hall ;   260
And in the hall itself was such a feast
As never man had dream'd ; for every knight
Had whatsoever meat he long'd for served
By hands unseen ; and even as he said
Down in the cellars merry bloated things
Shoulder'd the spigot, straddling on the butts
While the wine ran : so glad were spirits and men
Before the coming of the sinful Queen.'

Then spake the Queen and somewhat bitterly,
'Were they so glad? ill prophets were they all,   270
Spirits and men : could none of them foresee,
Not even thy wise father with his signs
And wonders, what has fall'n upon the realm?'

To whom the novice garrulously again,
'Yea, one, a bard ; of whom my father said,
Full many a noble war-song had he sung,
Ev'n in the presence of an enemy's fleet,
Between the steep cliff and the coming wave ;
And many a mystic lay of life and death
Had chanted on the smoky mountain-tops,   280
When round him bent the spirits of the hills
With all their dewy hair blown back like flame :
So said my father—and that night the bard
Sang Arthur's glorious wars, and sang the King
As wellnigh more than man, and rail'd at those
Who call'd him the false son of Gorloïs :
For there was no man knew from whence he came ;
But after tempest, when the long wave broke
All down the thundering shores of Bude and Bos,
There came a day as still as heaven, and then   290
They found a naked child upon the sands
Of dark Tintagil by the Cornish sea ;
And that was Arthur ; and they foster'd him

Till he by miracle was approven King:
And that his grave should be a mystery
From all men, like his birth; and could he find
A woman in her womanhood as great
As he was in his manhood, then, he sang,
The twain together well might change the world.
But even in the middle of his song   300
He falter'd, and his hand fell from the harp,
And pale he turn'd, and reel'd, and would have fall'n,
But that they stay'd him up; nor would he tell
His vision; but what doubt that he foresaw
This evil work of Lancelot and the Queen?'

Then thought the Queen, 'Lo! they have set her on,
Our simple-seeming Abbess and her nuns,
To play upon me,' and bow'd her head nor spake.
Whereat the novice crying, with clasp'd hands,
Shame on her own garrulity garrulously,   310
Said the good nuns would check her gadding tongue
Full often, 'and, sweet lady, if I seem
To vex an ear too sad to listen to me,
Unmannerly, with prattling and the tales
Which my good father told me, check me too
Nor let me shame my father's memory, one
Of noblest manners, tho' himself would say
Sir Lancelot had the noblest; and he died,
Kill'd in a tilt, come next, five summers back,
And left me; but of others who remain,   320
And of the two first-famed for courtesy—
And pray you check me if I ask amiss—
But pray you, which had noblest, while you moved
Among them, Lancelot or our lord the King?'

Then the pale Queen look'd up and answer'd her,
'Sir Lancelot, as became a noble knight,
Was gracious to all ladies, and the same

In open battle or the tilting-field
Forbore his own advantage, and the King
In open battle or the tilting-field   330
Forbore his own advantage, and these two
Were the most nobly-manner'd men of all;
For manners are not idle, but the fruit
Of loyal nature, and of noble mind.'

'Yea,' said the maid, 'be manners such fair fruit?
Then Lancelot's needs must be a thousand-fold
Less noble, being, as all rumour runs,
The most disloyal friend in all the world.'

To which a mournful answer made the Queen:
'O closed about by narrowing nunnery-walls,   340
What knowest thou of the world, and all its lights
And shadows, all the wealth and all the woe?
If ever Lancelot, that most noble knight,
Were for one hour less noble than himself,
Pray for him that he scape the doom of fire,
And weep for her who drew him to his doom.'

'Yea,' said the little novice, 'I pray for both;
But I should all as soon believe that his,
Sir Lancelot's, were as noble as the King's,
As I could think, sweet lady, yours would be   350
Such as they are, were you the sinful Queen.'

So she, like many another babbler, hurt
Whom she would soothe, and harm'd where she would
          heal;
For here a sudden flush of wrathful heat
Fired all the pale face of the Queen, who cried,
'Such as thou art be never maiden more
For ever! thou their tool, set on to plague
And play upon, and harry me, petty spy.

And traitress.' When that storm of anger brake
From Guinevere, aghast the maiden rose,   360
White as her veil, and stood before the Queen
As tremulously as foam upon the beach
Stands in a wind, ready to break and fly,
And when the Queen had added 'Get thee hence,'
Fled frighted. Then that other left alone
Sigh'd, and began to gather heart again,
Saying in herself, 'The simple, fearful child
Meant nothing, but my own too-fearful guilt,
Simpler than any child, betrays itself.
But help me, heaven, for surely I repent.   ·   370
For what is true repentance but in thought—
Not ev'n in inmost thought to think again
The sins that made the past so pleasant to us:
And I have sworn never to see him more,
To see him more.'

    And ev'n in saying this,
Her memory from old habit of the mind
Went slipping back upon the golden days
In which she saw him first, when Lancelot came,
Reputed the best knight and goodliest man,
Ambassador, to lead her to his lord   380
Arthur, and led her forth, and far ahead
Of his and her retinue moving, they,
Rapt in sweet talk or lively, all on love
And sport and tilts and pleasure, (for the time
Was maytime, and as yet no sin was dream'd,)
Rode under groves that look'd a paradise
Of blossom, over sheets of hyacinth
That seem'd the heavens upbreaking thro' the earth,
And on from hill to hill, and every day
Beheld at noon in some delicious dale   390
The silk pavilions of King Arthur raised
For brief repast or afternoon repose

By couriers gone before ; and on again,
Till yet once more ere set of sun they saw
The Dragon of the great Pendragonship,
That crown'd the state pavilion of the King,
Blaze by the rushing brook or silent well.

But when the Queen immersed in such a trance,
And moving thro' the past unconsciously,
Came to that point where first she saw the King 400
Ride toward her from the city, sigh'd to find
Her journey done, glanced at him, thought him cold,
High, self-contain'd, and passionless, not like him,
'Not like my Lancelot'—while she brooded thus
And grew half-guilty in her thoughts again,
There rode an armed warrior to the doors.
A murmuring whisper thro' the nunnery ran,
Then on a sudden a cry, 'The King.' She sat
Stiff-stricken, listening ; but when armed feet
Thro' the long gallery from the outer doors 410
Rang coming, prone from off her seat she fell,
And grovell'd with her face against the floor :
There with her milkwhite arms and shadowy hair
She made her face a darkness from the King :
And in the darkness heard his armed feet
Pause by her ; then came silence, then a voice,
Monotonous and hollow like a Ghost's
Denouncing judgment, but tho' changed, the King's :

'Liest thou here so low, the child of one
I honour'd, happy, dead before thy shame ? 420
Well is it that no child is born of thee.
The children born of thee are sword and fire,
Red ruin, and the breaking up of laws,
The craft of kindred and the Godless hosts
Of heathen swarming o'er the Northern Sea ;
Whom I, while yet Sir Lancelot, my right arm,

The mightiest of my knights, abode with me,
Have everywhere about this land of Christ
In twelve great battles ruining overthrown.
And knowest thou now from whence I come—from
    him,   430
From waging bitter war with him: and he,
That did not shun to smite me in worse way,
Had yet that grace of courtesy in him left,
He spared to lift his hand against the King
Who made him knight: but many a knight was slain;
And many more, and all his kith and kin
Clave to him, and abode in his own land.
And many more when Modred raised revolt,
Forgetful of their troth and fealty, clave
To Modred, and a remnant stays with me.   440
And of this remnant will I leave a part,
True men who love me still, for whom I live,
To guard thee in the wild hour coming on,
Lest but a hair of this low head be harm'd.
Fear not: thou shalt be guarded till my death.
Howbeit I know, if ancient prophecies
Have err'd not, that I march to meet my doom.
Thou hast not made my life so sweet to me,
That I the King should greatly care to live;
For thou hast spoilt the purpose of my life.   450
Bear with me for the last time while I show,
Ev'n for thy sake, the sin which thou hast sinn'd.
For when the Roman left us, and their law
Relax'd its hold upon us, and the ways
Were fill'd with rapine, here and there a deed
Of prowess done redress'd a random wrong.
But I was first of all the kings who drew
The knighthood-errant of this realm and all
The realms together under me, their Head,
In that fair Order of my Table Round,   460
A glorious company, the flower of men,

To serve as model for the mighty world,
And be the fair beginning of a time.
I made them lay their hands in mine and swear
To reverence the King, as if he were
Their conscience, and their conscience as their King,
To break the heathen and uphold the Christ,
To ride abroad redressing human wrongs,
To speak no slander, no, nor listen to it,
To honour his own word as if his God's, 470
To lead sweet lives in purest chastity,
To love one maiden only, cleave to her,
And worship her by years of noble deeds,
Until they won her; for indeed I knew
Of no more subtle master under heaven
Than is the maiden passion for a maid,
Not only to keep down the base in man,
But teach high thought, and amiable words
And courtliness, and the desire of fame,
And love of truth, and all that makes a man. 480
And all this throve before I wedded thee,
Believing, "lo mine helpmate, one to feel
My purpose and rejoicing in my joy."
Then came thy shameful sin with Lancelot;
Then came the sin of Tristram and Isolt;
Then others, following these my mightiest knights,
And drawing foul ensample from fair names,
Sinn'd also, till the loathsome opposite
Of all my heart had destined did obtain,
And all thro' thee! so that this life of mine 490
I guard as God's high gift from scathe and wrong,
Not greatly care to lose; but rather think
How sad it were for Arthur, should he live,   .
To sit once more within his lonely hall,
And miss the wonted number of my knights,
And miss to hear high talk of noble deeds
As in the golden days before thy sin.

For which of us, who might be left, could speak
Of the pure heart, nor seem to glance at thee?
And in thy bowers of Camelot or of Usk   500
Thy shadow still would glide from room to room,
And I should evermore be vext with thee
In hanging robe or vacant ornament,
Or ghostly footfall echoing on the stair.
For think not, tho' thou wouldst not love thy lord,
Thy lord has wholly lost his love for thee.
I am not made of so slight elements.
Yet must I leave thee, woman, to thy shame.
I hold that man the worst of public foes
Who either for his own or children's sake,   510
To save his blood from scandal, lets the wife
Whom he knows false, abide and rule the house:
For being thro' his cowardice allow'd
Her station, taken everywhere for pure,
She like a new disease, unknown to men,
Creeps, no precaution used, among the crowd,
Makes wicked lightnings of her eyes, and saps
The fealty of our friends, and stirs the pulse
With devil's leaps, and poisons half the young.   519
Worst of the worst were that man he that reigns!
Better the King's waste hearth and aching heart
Than thou reseated in thy place of light,
The mockery of my people, and their bane.'

  He paused, and in the pause she crept an inch
Nearer, and laid her hands about his feet.
Far off a solitary trumpet blew.
Then waiting by the doors the warhorse neigh'd
As at a friend's voice, and he spake again:

  'Yet think not that I come to urge thy crimes,
I did not come to curse thee, Guinevere,   530
I, whose vast pity almost makes me die

To see thee, laying there thy golden head,
My pride in happier summers, at my feet.
The wrath which forced my thoughts on that fierce
    law,
The doom of treason and the flaming death,
(When first I learnt thee hidden here) is past.
The pang—which while I weigh'd thy heart with one
Too wholly true to dream untruth in thee,
Made my tears burn—is also past—in part.
And all is past, the sin is sinn'd, and I,   540
Lo! I forgive thee, as Eternal God
Forgives: do thou for thine own soul the rest.
But how to take last leave of all I loved?
O golden hair, with which I used to play
Not knowing! O imperial-moulded form,
And beauty such as never woman wore,
Until it came a kingdom's curse with thee—
I cannot touch thy lips, they are not mine,
But Lancelot's: nay, they never were the King's.
I cannot take thy hand; that too is flesh,   550
And in the flesh thou hast sinn'd; and mine own flesh,
Here looking down on thine polluted, cries
"I loathe thee:" yet not less, O Guinevere,
For I was ever virgin save for thee,
My love thro' flesh hath wrought into my life
So far, that my doom is, I love thee still.
Let no man dream but that I love thee still.
Perchance, and so thou purify thy soul,
And so thou lean on our fair father Christ,
Hereafter in that world where all are pure   560
We two may meet before high God, and thou
Wilt spring to me, and claim me thine, and know
I am thine husband—not a smaller soul,
Nor Lancelot, nor another. Leave me that,
I charge thee, my last hope. Now must I hence.
Thro' the thick night I hear the trumpet blow:

B

They summon me their King to lead mine hosts
Far down to that great battle in the west,
Where I must strike against the man they call
My sister's son—no kin of mine, who leagues   570
With Lords of the White Horse, heathen, and knights,
Traitors—and strike him dead, and meet myself
Death, or I know not what mysterious doom.
And thou remaining here wilt learn the event;
But hither shall I never come again,
Never lie by thy side; see thee no more—
Farewell!'

            And while she grovell'd at his feet,
She felt the King's breath wander o'er her neck,
And in the darkness o'er her fallen head,
Perceived the waving of his hands that blest.   580

    Then, listening till those armed steps were gone,
Rose the pale Queen, and in her anguish found
The casement: 'peradventure,' so she thought,
'If I might see his face, and not be seen.'
And lo, he sat on horseback at the door!
And near him the sad nuns with each a light
Stood, and he gave them charge about the Queen,
To guard and foster her for evermore.
And while he spake to these his helm was lower'd,
To which for crest the golden dragon clung   590
Of Britain; so she did not see the face,
Which then was as an angel's, but she saw,
Wet with the mists and smitten by the lights,
The Dragon of the great Pendragonship
Blaze, making all the night a steam of fire.
And even then he turn'd; and more and more
The moony vapour rolling round the King,
Who seem'd the phantom of a Giant in it,
Enwound him fold by fold, and made him gray

And grayer, till himself became as mist 600
Before her, moving ghostlike to his doom.

Then she stretch'd out her arms and cried aloud
'Oh Arthur!' there her voice brake suddenly,
Then—as a stream that spouting from a cliff
Fails in mid air, but gathering at the base
Re-makes itself, and flashes down the vale—
Went on in passionate utterance:

     'Gone—my lord!
Gone thro' my sin to slay and to be slain!
And he forgave me, and I could not speak.
Farewell? I should have answer'd his farewell. 610
His mercy choked me. Gone, my lord the King,
My own true lord! how dare I call him mine?
The shadow of another cleaves to me,
And makes me one pollution: he, the King,
Call'd me polluted: shall I kill myself?
What help in that? I cannot kill my sin,
If soul be soul; nor can I kill my shame;
No, nor by living can I live it down.
The days will grow to weeks, the weeks to months,
The months will add themselves and make the years,
The years will roll into the centuries, 621
And mine will ever be a name of scorn.
I must not dwell on that defeat of fame.
Let the world be; that is but of the world.
What else? what hope? I think there was a hope,
Except he mock'd me when he spake of hope;
His hope he call'd it; but he never mocks,
For mockery is the fume of little hearts.
And blessed be the King, who hath forgiven
My wickedness to him, and left me hope 630
That in mine own heart I can live down sin
And be his mate hereafter in the heavens

Before high God. Ah great and gentle lord,
Who wast, as is the conscience of a saint
Among his warring senses, to thy knights—
To whom my false voluptuous pride, that took
Full easily all impressions from below,
Would not look up, or half-despised the height
To which I would not or I could not climb—
I thought I could not breathe in that fine air   640
That pure severity of perfect light—
I yearn'd for warmth and colour which I found
In Lancelot—now I see thee what thou art,
Thou art the highest and most human too,
Not Lancelot, nor another. Is there none
Will tell the King I love him tho' so late?
Now—ere he goes to the great Battle? none:
Myself must tell him in that purer life,
But now it were too daring. Ah my God,
What might I not have made of thy fair world,   650
Had I but loved thy highest creature here?
It was my duty to have loved the highest:
It surely was my profit had I known:
It would have been my pleasure had I seen.
We needs must love the highest when we see it,
Not Lancelot, nor another.'

                              Here her hand
Grasp'd, made her vail her eyes: she looked and saw
The novice, weeping, suppliant, and said to her,
'Yea, little maid, for am *I* not forgiven?'
Then glancing up beheld the holy nuns   660
All round her, weeping; and her heart was loosed
Within her, and she wept with these and said,

      'Ye know me then, that wicked one, who broke
The vast design and purpose of the King.
O shut me round with narrowing nunnery-walls,

Meek maidens, from the voices crying "shame."
I must not scorn myself : he loves me still.
Let no one dream but that he loves me still.
So let me, if you do not shudder at me,
Nor shun to call me sister, dwell with you ;   670
Wear black and white, and be a nun like you,
Fast with your fasts, not feasting with your feasts ;
Grieve with your griefs, not grieving at your joys,
But not rejoicing ; mingle with your rites ;
Pray and be pray'd for ; lie before your shrines ;
Do each low office of your holy house ;
Walk your dim cloister, and distribute dole
To poor sick people, richer in His eyes
Who ransom'd us, and haler too than I ;
And treat their loathsome hurts and heal mine own ;
And so wear out in almsdeed and in prayer   681
The sombre close of that voluptuous day,
Which wrought the ruin of my lord the King.'

      She. said : they took her to themselves ; and she
Still hoping, fearing 'is it yet too late ?'
Dwelt with them, till in time their Abbess died. .
Then she, for her good deeds and her pure life,
And for the power of ministration in her,
And likewise for the high rank she had borne,
Was chosen Abbess, there, an Abbess, lived   690
For three brief years, and there, an Abbess, past
To where beyond these voices there is peace.

NOTES.

1. **Queen Guinevere had fled the court**, etc. This manner of beginning, by which there is presented to us at once a picture, as it were, of the persons concerned or of the situation, and then there follows an explanation, is very usual with Tennyson, and it may probably have seemed to him the most suitable arrangement for an 'idyll.' We find it also in *The Marriage of Geraint, Merlin and Vivien, Lancelot and Elaine, Pelleas and Ettarre*, and *The Last Tournament*. Here the picture is contained in the first eight lines, the explanation in ll. 9-180, and then the story is resumed at the point from which the poem began. At the same time, now that the idyll of *Guinevere* no longer stands alone, but is linked with the rest of the series, we must not forget the connexion of these opening words with the conclusion of *The Last Tournament* :

> " That night came Arthur home, and while he climb'd,
> All in a death-dumb autumn-dripping gloom,
> The stairway to the hall, and look'd and saw
> The great Queen's bower was dark,—about his feet
> A voice clung sobbing till he question'd it,
> ' What art thou ?' and the voice about his feet
> Sent up an answer, sobbing, ' I am thy fool,
> And I shall never make thee smile again.' "

2. **the holy house at Almesbury.** Almesbury or Amesbury is in Wiltshire, about seven miles from Salisbury. It had once a house of Benedictine nuns, and it was supposed that there had been a more ancient British monastery at the same place, called, as some said, after King Ambrosius ('Ambrosebury') who was there buried. The later Benedictine foundation became at one time a favourite place of retreat for ladies of high rank. Mary, daughter of King Edward I. took the veil there in 1285, and two years afterwards Eleanor, the mother of the same king, herself retired to the same house (Dugdale, *Monasticon*, ii. p. 334).

3. **Weeping.** The immediate occasion of this weeping is given afterwards, ll. 150-180.

4. **A novice,** *i.e.* one who had entered the convent, but had not yet taken the final vows which would bind her for life.

5. **Blurr'd by the creeping mist,** etc. External nature sympathizes with the action throughout the *Idylls of the King*, and the progress of the events is to some extent typified by the succession of the seasons in a year, while Arthur runs his course almost like the ' Sun in heaven ' to which he is compared by Guinevere (see note on l. 402). The birth or coming of Arthur takes place on ' the night of the new year '; his marriage and coronation in May. The idyll of *Gareth and Lynette* belongs to the spring, and Arthur is then still in the spring-time of his glory. *The Marriage of Geraint, Geraint and Enid, Lancelot and Elaine,* and *The Holy Grail* are all idylls of the summer. *The Last Tournament* and *Guinevere* are of autumn; while *The Passing of Arthur* belongs to the very last days of the dying year,

> " when the great light of heaven
> Burn'd at his lowest in the rolling year."

After Arthur has finally passed away from the sight of Bedivere, the new sun rises "bringing the new year" and with it a new cycle of human endeavour. Here the death of Arthur and the failure of his purpose seem to be typified in the mist which obscures the sun and lies upon the earth as a face-cloth upon the face of the dead, penetrating even into the chamber where the guilty queen and her little novice sat, and dimming the light that burned between them. So also in *The Passing of Arthur* :

> " A deathwhite mist slept over sand and sea :
> Whereof the chill, to him who breathed it, drew
> Down with his blood, till all his heart was cold
> With formless fear."

The word ' blurr'd ' means dimmed.

all abroad, everywhere over the land.

6. **albeit,** ' although.'

7. **like a face-cloth,** etc. As a face-cloth clings to the face of the corpse, so the white mist clung to the face of the dead earth. The word ' dead ' in the next line suggests the main idea that is intended in the comparison.

Observe the variety of pauses in the above quite simple passage of eight lines. It is worth noticing that the blank verse of Tennyson is far more varied generally in the distribution of pauses than (for example) that of Milton.

10. **Sir Modred.** The Modred of the *Idylls* is the son of Lot, king of Orkney, and of Bellicent, daughter of Gorloïs and

Ygerne. Gawain and Gareth are his brothers. In the first
edition of *Guinevere* he is here called Arthur's nephew,

"He, the nearest to the King,
His nephew, ever like a subtle beast
Lay couchant," etc.

This has been since altered by the omission of the words 'the
nearest to the King, His nephew,' and a similar alteration has
been made later in l. 569, where the first edition has—

"Where I must strike against my sister's son,
Leagued with the Lords of the White Horse and knights
Once mine, and strike him dead," etc.

The intention of these changes evidently is to avoid a definite
assertion on the mysterious question of Arthur's birth, and to
leave the suggestion of a supernatural origin to be accepted by
those who will. In the first of the Idylls, *The Coming of Arthur*,
we find set forth some of the "many rumours on this head," the
opinion of his loyal knights, that he was son of Uther and
Ygerne, and the story of Bellicent about the dragon ship seen
high upon the sea at Tintagil, and the naked babe borne by
a great wave to Merlin's feet.

On the occasion when this tale was told Bellicent was
visiting King Leodogran, the father of Guinevere, at Cameliard,
accompanied by her sons, 'Gawain and young Modred,' and
the character of Modred is indicated in contrast to that
of Gawain by his action of staying beside the doors to listen
to that which his mother has to tell the king. In *Gareth and
Lynette* his youngest brother, Gareth, speaks of him with contempt as envious and sullen, again in contrast to Gawain. So in
this idyll he is represented as an eavesdropper, and as one who
makes a pretended regard for the king's honour instrumental
in furthering his own treasonable ends.

In the romances Modred (or Mordred) is a less contemptible
character, but he is treacherous and malicious, and he has
a special spite against Lancelot. In some, as for example,
Malory's *Morte Darthur*, he is represented as the son of Arthur.

11. **Lay couchant.** The metaphor is of a beast of prey, a
panther or a leopard, couching for a spring, with its eyes
fixed upon its prey. Elsewhere, as in l. 62, Modred is compared
to a fox, but here it is not only craft and subtlety that is
suggested, but also especially the dangerous spring upon the
object of his desires. Notice the form of the comparison, in
which simile and metaphor are combined, as they are naturally
apt to be.

Mr. Littledale (*Essays on Tennyson's Idylls of the King*) quotes
as a 'curious coincidence' the use of the same metaphor in some
lines by Arthur Hallam on Tennyson himself—

> " whose fame
> Is couching now with panther eyes intent,
> As who shall say, ' I'll spring to him anon,
> And have him for my own.' "

Couchant is originally a French word used in heraldry, as passant, rampant, gardant, volant, to describe the position or action of animals represented in coats of arms or crests..

12. **for this,** that is, to prepare the opportunity for his ambition.

14. **With silent smiles,** etc. Modred listens to the popular praises of Arthur in silence, and with a smile which implies contempt of that which he hears, or superior knowledge, and so gradually chills the enthusiasm of the speakers. The epithet ' slow ' marks the difference between this result and the sudden check caused by open opposition.

disparagement is properly offering indignity so as to lower a person in rank, from the old French *parage*, lineage, rank, and so, as here, depreciation (Skeat, *Etym. Dict.*). Pope's well-known lines on this kind of disparagement are worth quoting both for their likeness to the present passage and their differences from it :

> " Should such a man, too fond to rule alone,
> Bear, like the Turk, no brother near his throne,
>
> Damn with faint praise, assent with civil leer,
> And without sneering, teach the rest to sneer ;
> Willing to wound and yet afraid to strike,
> Just hint a fault and hesitate dislike ;
>
> Who but must laugh, if such a man there be ?
> Who would not weep, if Atticus were he ? "
> —*Prologue to the Satires*, 197 ff.

15. **tamper'd with.** The word 'tamper' means originally to deal or meddle with a person or a thing, cf. ' temper '; but it has acquired a bad sense and means to meddle in a wrongful way or so as to spoil and corrupt. Here the idea is of wrongful and treasonable dealing with those who were the enemies of his king.

the Lords of the White Horse are the heathen Saxons, against whom Arthur had waged war. The white horse was the emblem of the Saxons or English, as the dragon of the Britons and the raven of the Danes. The names of Hengist and Horsa, the two leaders under whom the Saxons, or rather perhaps the Jutes, are said to have first established themselves in Britain, mean ' horse ' and ' marc,' and the Saxon practice of cutting out white horses on slopes of the chalk downs in England is well known. A familiar example is that which commemorates the

victory of Ashdown, gained by the English under Alfred over
the Danes in the year 871. In *Lancelot and Elaine*, where the
twelve battles of Arthur against the heathen are enumerated,
the 'white Horse' again represents the Saxon power :

> " When the strong neighings of the wild white Horse
> Set every gilded parapet shuddering " (l. 297-8).

Tacitus, in describing the manner of divination practised by the
Germans, says as follows :
" It is a peculiar practice of this race also to take presages and
warnings from horses.   These, which are white in colour and
subject to no ordinary work, are kept at the public expense in
sacred groves, and when they have been harnessed to a sacred
chariot, the priest or the king or the chief of the state accom-
panies them and observes their neighings and snortings.   No
kind of omen is in greater credit than this, and that not only
with the people, but with the nobles and the priests ; for these
say that they themselves are the ministers of the gods, but the
horses are privy to their designs " (*Germania*, 10).
In fact the white horse was a sacred animal with the German
race in general.

16. **the brood by Hengist left** : that is, the descendants of
Hengist and of his followers.   The word 'brood,' when used
metaphorically, has usually a bad sense attached to it ; so in
Milton, *Par. Lost*, ii. 862 f. :

> " With terrors and with clamours compassed round
> Of mine own brood that on my bowels feed."

17. **disruption**, from Lat. *dis-ruptio*, ' a breaking asunder.'

the Table Round : that is the company or order of knights
called of the Round Table.   Some romances say that the
Round Table itself was presented by King Leodogran, father
of Guinevere, to Arthur on his marriage.   It had places for a
hundred and fifty knights, and Leodogran sent a hundred,
bidding Arthur fill up the remaining fifty places ; but Merlin
left two places void, the Siege Perilous and another.   This
version of the story is told in Malory's *Morte Darthur*, iii. 1,
from the French *Roman de Merlin* ; but later (*Morte Darthur*,
xiv. 2), where the compiler is following the *Roman de Lancelot*,
we are told that Merlin made the Round Table in token of the
roundness of the world, "for all the world, Christian and heathen,
repair unto the Round Table."   And he made one place at it
where he only might sit who should pass all other knights, and
this was the Siege Perilous, in which Galahad at length sat.   At
Whitsuntide each year was held the high feast of the Table
Round, at which the number of the knights was made up to the
full tale.

Other legends, however, say that the Round Table was made after the model of that used by Christ and his disciples at the Last Supper, and had thirteen seats, of which one, corresponding to that used by Christ himself, was left vacant.

Reference should be made to ll. 457 ff. of this present idyll for Arthur's own account of the foundation of his Order, of its objects, and of the oath taken by the knights. The idea of an Order of Chivalry such as is described in the Arthur romances, belongs to the thirteenth and fourteenth centuries, at which period such institutions flourished. The English Order of the Garter was founded in direct imitation of the Round Table of the romances.

A table called Arthur's Round Table is preserved at Winchester, and is mentioned by Caxton in the preface to the *Morte Darthur*, in company with Gawain's skull, Cradok's mantle, and Lancelot's sword, as one of the relics which make Arthur's historical existence undeniable.

18. **splinter it into feuds.** The hurrying of the rhythm gives additional effect to the word ' splinter.' ' Feud ' means properly hatred, from Anglo-Saxon *fáh*, hostile, whence comes the modern English 'foe' (Skeat, *Etym. Dict.*).

20. **strong hate for Lancelot.** In the romances this hatred of Modred and his brother Agravaine for Lancelot is justified to some extent by jealousy for Arthur's reputation. Here the poet, desiring to deprive Modred of all the reader's sympathies, ascribes the feeling to petty rancour arising out of a casual offence.

22. **mock'd the may,** that is, were as white as the may-blossom. The word 'mock,' from meaning to mutter or to make derisive sounds with the lips, comes to mean to imitate in derision and hence simply to imitate.

23. **their wont,** 'as was their custom,' the words being in apposition to the words ' Had been ... a-maying.'

a-maying, originally 'on maying,' as we have it in the *Morte Darthur*, xix. 1, where such an occasion is described : "So it befell in the month of May queen Guenever called unto her knights of the Table Round, and she gave them warning that early upon the morning she would ride on maying into the woods and fields beside Westminster. And I warn you that there be none of you but that he be well horsed, and that ye all be clothed in green, other in silk other in cloth, and I shall bring with me ten ladies, and every knight shall have a lady behind him, and every knight shall have a squire and two yeomen, and I will that ye all be well horsed.... And so upon the morn they took their horses, with the queen, and rode on maying in woods and meadows, as it pleased them, in great joy and delights."

The twentieth book of the *Morte Darthur* also begins with the month of May: "In May, when every lusty heart flourisheth and burgeneth," etc., placing at that time the discovery of the love of Lancelot and Guinevere, and the final catastrophe, with the death of Arthur and Modred, on the Monday after Trinity Sunday. Tennyson does not miss the opening note, but he connects it only with a preliminary incident, and the discovery and catastrophe belong to the close of the year. Notice that in the *Coming of Arthur* May is the month of the marriage and solemn coronation of Arthur:

> "Far shone the fields of May thro' open door,
> The sacred altar blossom'd white with May,
> The Sun of May descended on their King" (459 ff.).

26. **scandal**, 'disgrace' or 'shameful deed,' originally from Greek σκάνδαλον, a snare or stumbling-block, hence of that which causes offence.

27. **her best, Enid.** Enid, as she appears in *The Marriage of Geraint* and *Geraint and Enid* is the simplest and purest ideal of maiden and of wife that Tennyson has presented to us. She is loved by Guinevere, and is the loveliest in all the court next after the queen herself:

> "And Enid loved the Queen, and with true heart
> Adored her, as the stateliest and the best
> And loveliest of all women upon earth."
> *Marriage of Geraint*, 19 ff.

The idylls of *Enid* and *Vivien* were originally printed privately with the title *Enid and Nimue, or the True and the False*, and he no doubt selected the two characters as a contrast, and they are brought in here in the same way as types of the best and the worst, the 'heaven and hell' of female character.

28. **lissome Vivien.** The word 'lissome' is for 'lithesome,' from 'lithe' meaning pliant, flexible. The epithet belongs to Vivien also in the idyll of *Merlin and Vivien*. Of her it seems to be used in a rather bad sense, implying some moral characteristics in harmony with the physical; but not so always, e.g. *The Brook*, 70:

> "Straight, but as lissome as a hazel wand."

The Vivien of Tennyson has nothing to do with the Lady of the Lake, the foster-mother of Lancelot, with whom her representative in the romances is identified. She appears first at the court of King Mark of Cornwall. Her father has fallen in battle against Arthur, and her mother has died upon his corpse in the open field, where she herself was born. She scorns the supposed purity of Arthur's court, and undertakes to "ferret out their burrowings," and then to return to Mark. She goes and throws herself at the feet of Guinevere with a piteous tale imploring protection, and so taking her place at the court of the queen,

> "Among her damsels broidering sat, heard, watch'd
> And whisper'd : thro' the peaceful court she crept
> And whisper'd : then as Arthur in the highest
> Leaven'd the world, so Vivien in the lowest,
> Arriving at a time of golden rest,
> And sowing one ill hint from ear to ear,
> While all the heathen lay at Arthur's feet,
> And no quest came, but all was joust and play,
> Leaven'd his hall."
>
> *—Merlin and Vivien,* 136 ff.

Thereafter follows the story of the wiles by which she at length succeeded in casting a spell upon Merlin and enclosing him as dead within a hollow oak.

The account referred to above of the manner of Vivien's coming to Arthur's court is an addition made when the idyll of *Vivien* was incorporated with the rest under the title of *Merlin and Vivien,* and in accordance with this account we find in this idyll the added touch,

> "Vivien, lurking, heard.
> She told Sir Modred " (l. 97).

In the idyll of *Balin and Balan* we see Vivien apparently on her way from the court of Mark to that of Arthur, riding through the woods near Camelot.

29. **willest**: derived from 'wile,' meaning a trick, device, of which 'guile' is a doublet.

31. **as the gardener's hand,** etc. Note the characteristic exactness of the simile. Where another poet might be satisfied with the general likeness of the plucking down and casting upon the ground, Tennyson works out the details of the resemblance, hinting at the colour of Modred's suit, and not leaving out the flowering grasses, from among which he was plucked. This kind of work, so minutely and elaborately picturesque, is evidently more suitable to the idyllic than to the epic style.

32. **colewort** is simply cabbage : 'cole' from Latin *caulis* and 'wort,' English for 'plant.'

33. **the flowering grove Of grasses :** This picturesque addition adds to the completeness of the simile. Modred, like the caterpillar, is plucked from the flowering herbage.

36. **marr'd,** properly 'injured' or 'spoilt': hence of the appearance being disfigured. So in *Geraint and Enid,* 550 :

> "Ye mar a comely face with idiot tears."

Cf. *Lancelot and Elaine,* 246 ff.

37. king's blood: because, whether he were really akin to Arthur or no, he was reputed to be so. Also his father Lot was a king.

in a bad man, that is, though the man in whose veins it ran was unworthy.

39. Full knightly, 'in true knightly and courteous fashion': so *Lancelot and Elaine*, 236:

"Full courtly, yet not falsely, thus return'd."

40. No knight of Arthur's noblest, etc. Compare the account given by Edyrn in *Geraint and Enid*, ll. 855-863, of his reception at the court:

"Where first as sullen as a beast new caged,
And waiting to be treated as a wolf,
Because I knew my deeds were known, I found,
Instead of scornful pity or pure scorn,
Such fine reserve and noble reticence,
Manners so kind, yet stately, such a grace
Of tenderest courtesy, that I began
To glance behind me at my former life,
And find that it had been the wolf's indeed."

41. halt or hunch'd, 'lame or humpbacked,' opposed to "full-limb'd and tall" in the next line.

43. A certain bitterness of spirit, expressing itself in scornful gibes, is popularly thought to accompany deformity of body. Thersites in Homer is described as halt and hunched (φολκὸς ἔην, χωλὸς δ' ἔτερον πόδα), and at the same time reckless in speech (ἀκριτόμυθος), but he was certainly not treated with the forbearance which is here described.

45. holp: the strong form of the past tense is often preferred by Tennyson in the words help, climb, and a few others, but the truer form in this case would be 'halp.'

47. smote his knees, to shake off the dust.

smiled, to hide his rancour, the "heart-hiding smile" of l. 63.

49. Rankled. The verb 'to rankle' means properly to fester, from 'rank' in its later sense of rancid, or strong-smelling (Skeat, *Etym. Dict.*). The metaphor is completely changed in the succeeding words.

50. As the sharp wind, etc. One of Tennyson's most graphic and forcible similes. The picture is perfect in the first place, of the little pool of salt water round a stone on the barren coast, a pool which by reason of its shallowness is the more easily ruffled by every wind that passes over it; and its every detail suggests something in the person referred to, the coldness and hardness, and at the same time the shallowness and bitterness, of his nature.

51. bitter, because made of salt water left by the tide.

55. Then shudder'd, as the village wife, etc. The idea is of an involuntary shudder for no obvious cause, which by popular superstition would be attributed to some cause such as is here suggested. The queen's first shudder is from an unreasoning impulse : afterwards she half-foresees the actual danger to be apprehended.

61. front, 'face,' not quite the same as " daily fronted him," in *Marriage of Geraint*, 13, where the word means simply 'came before him': here it has the idea of looking straight in a person's face.

hall, the banqueting-hall of the knights.

62. narrow foxy face : cf. *Last Tournament*, 164 ff. :

" And once the laces of a helmet crack'd,
    And show'd him, like a vermin in its hole,
    Modred, a narrow face."

63. persistent, because constantly fixed upon her.

65. the death that cannot die, that is, eternal death, the death that has no ending.

69. grim, 'fierce,' 'cruel': connected originally with words that mean to roar or to yell.

70. Scan the line thus :

" Befóre her, ór a vágue spíritual feár,"

making a slight pause after 'vague,' and reading the first syllables of ' spiritual' as a dactyl, with stress on the first. Cf. l. 211 :

" Then to her own sad heart mutter'd the Queen."

Spiritual seems here to mean ghostly or supernatural.

72. the watcher is simply the person who lies awake.

73. the rust of murder is an expressive phrase for stains upon the walls of old houses, which might popularly be supposed to be the marks of blood or indicative in some way of murders committed there.

75. It is easy to read the interpretation of the dream. The setting sun is Arthur, and the " ghastly something," which comes from thence towards her till its shadow touches her, is the dreaded discovery of her guilt. Then, turning to flee, she sees that behind her back her own shadow cuts off from all the

land the light of the sinking sun, and the darkness is only
broken by the fires of burning cities; for she has spoilt the
purpose of Arthur's life, and through her the land is to return to
its former state of war and devastation, as pictured in the dream
of Leodogran her father before she was wedded to Arthur (see
Coming of Arthur, 426 ff.).

Tennyson is fond of introducing prophetic dreams. We have
in the *Idylls*, besides that which has been just mentioned, the
dreams of Enid, of Pelleas, of Tristram, and that of Arthur
himself before the last great battle.

78. **ghastly**, 'terrible.' The older form is 'gastly,' connected
with 'gasten,' to terrify. There is no connexion with the word
'ghost.'

84. Every indication of Arthur's peace of mind with regard to
her and trust in her became a torment to her.

86. **bane**, 'hurt,' originally meaning 'destruction,' from Anglo-
Saxon *bana*, a murderer.

87. Lancelot's "own land" was 'Benwick,' of which his father
Ban had been king. The author of the *Morte Darthur* says,
"Some men call it Bayonne and some men call it Beaume, where
the wine of Beaume is" (xx. 18).

90. **the smouldering scandal.** The metaphor is the same as in
the *Coming of Arthur*, 63 ff. :

"A doubt that ever smouldered in the hearts
Of those great Lords and Barons of his realm
Flash'd forth and into war." :

The queen refers to that "rumour" of her love for Lancelot
which we find referred to even in *Geraint and Enid*, and which
gathers strength as we go through the Idylls, until all the court
except Arthur himself seems to be aware of it.

94. **if thou love me.** It would be difficult to give any reason
for the use of the subjunctive here; but the subjunctive in
English has come to be so loosely employed, when employed at
all, that we cannot say definitely that such an expression as this
is incorrect. Shakspeare gives us : "No more of that, Hal, an
thou lovest me," 1 *Henry IV.* II. 4.

95. **upon a night ... to meet**, etc. That is, they appointed
a night on which to meet.

96. Arthur was absent on the expedition against the Red
Knight, who had established his Round Table in the North in
scorn of Arthur's ; see the *Last Tournament*, ll. 56-133, and also
the conclusion of the same idyll, where it is indicated that on
his return he found the queen gone. The place where these

events are supposed to occur is Camelot, as we learn also from the *Last Tournament*, l. 3, etc.

97. Vivien—Modred. This is an addition to the original poem, made to suit with the added introduction to *Vivien*, where we are told that Vivien came to Arthur's court for the express purpose of spying out scandal. These few words add great dramatic intensity to the part played by Vivien in the Idylls.

98. Passion-pale : cf. *Vision of Sin*, 18 :

" they that heard it sigh'd,
Panting hand in hand with faces pale."

99. Hands in hands, and eye to eye. The combination of plural and singular here is characteristic of the poet, who constantly avoids the common-place and seeks for variety. For a parallel to this whole scene see *Love and Duty*, 54 ff. :

" Could Love part thus? was it not well to speak,
To have spoken once? It could not but be well.
The slow sweet hours that bring us all things good,
The slow sad hours that bring us all things ill,
And all good things from evil, brought the night
In which we sat together and alone,
And to the want, that hollow'd all the heart,
Gave utterance by the yearning of an eye,
That burn'd upon its object thro' such tears
As flow but once a life.
                    The trance gave way
To those caresses, when a hundred times
In that last kiss, which never was the last,
Farewell, like endless welcome, lived and died."

103. His creatures, that is those whom he had suborned to help him. They are 'his creatures' in the sense that he makes them into instruments of his purpose.

104. For testimony, *i.e.* to bear witness to the fact that Lancelot was found in the queen's chamber.

105. trapt : so Tennyson writes 'past,' 'vext,' 'slipt,' 'drest,' 'fixt,' 'leapt,' for 'passed,' 'vexed,' 'slipped,' etc. It is an attempt at phonetic spelling, in which he is anticipated by Spenser, who writes also ' kist,' ' chaft,' ' chaunst,' etc.

107. Scan the line thus :

" Leápt on him, and húrl'd him héadlong," etc.

The dactylic rhythm suggests the action, as *e.g. Holy Grail*, 458 :

" In silver armour suddenly Galahad shone
Before us."

C

In the next line the position of the word 'Stunn'd,' at the beginning of the verse with a pause after it, is very effective : cf. *Geraint and Enid*, 388 f. :

> "jangling the casque
> Fell, and he started up and stared at her."

Holy Grail, 495 f. :

> " The lightnings here and there to left and right
> Struck."

111. **Mine be the shame**, 'let the shame be mine.'

112. **my strong castle overseas** : see note on l. 87. The castle of 'Joyous Gard,' to which the Lancelot of the romances carries Guinevere, was not overseas, but in the northern parts of Britain.

118. **Mine is the shame**, referring to Lancelot's words, " Mine be the shame," in l. 111.

120. **draw me**, 'withdraw myself.'

into sanctuary, that is into some convent or religious house, where she would be free from arrest.

121. **bide my doom**, 'await my sentence.'

123. **the divided way** : that is the place where the road leading to the convent at Almesbury diverged from that by which Lancelot was going to his own land.

125. We have the same line in *Lancelot and Elaine*, 89 :

> " a heart
> Love-loyal to the least wish of the Queen."

Similar repetitions occur several times in the *Idylls* and are no doubt intended to have something of an epic character. For example, the line :

> " But when the next day broke from underground,"

occurs (with slight variation) twice in *Lancelot and Elaine*, and twice in the *Holy Grail*. In this idyll we may note as of the same kind the repetitions in ll. 222-224, 330, 594, etc., and in the *Passing of Arthur* instances are frequent, that idyll having been published originally as a fragment of an epic. From this class of repetition we must distinguish those which either have pathetic intention, as,

> " I love thee still.
> Let no man dream but that I love thee still,"

or aim at enhancing the effect of simple words, such as the repetition of the word 'whisper'd' in the quotation from *Merlin and Vivien*, given in the note on l. 28.

127. **glimmering waste**. The epithet 'glimmering' expresses picturesquely the dim suggestions of light and shade which

landscape affords by night. It is rather a favourite word with Tennyson, as, *e.g.*:

> " where couch'd at ease
> The white kine glimmer'd " (in the twilight).
> — *In Memoriam*, xcv. 15.

> " The casement slowly grows a glimmering square "
> (to the eyes of a dying man).
> — *Princess*, iv. 34.

and in the fine simile of the breaking wave in *Lancelot and Elaine*, 481 :

> " Green-glimmering toward the summit."

In most of the instances the word suggests a dim or veiled light. Originally it is a frequentative of ' gleam.'

weald is properly ' forest,' cf. German *Wald.*

128. The repetition in this line is characteristic of the poet, and so also is that of the word ' moan ' in the next line.

131. **the cold wind that foreruns the morn :** cf. *In Memoriam*, xcv. 53 ff.:

> " And suck'd from out the distant gloom
> A breeze began to tremble o'er
> The large leaves of the sycamore,
> And fluctuate all the still perfume,

> " And gathering freshlier overhead,
> Rock'd the full-foliaged elms, and swung
> The heavy-folded rose, and flung
> The lilies to and fro, and said

> " ' The dawn, the dawn,' and died away."

132. **the Raven.** The word is given with a capital letter in all the editions, probably to indicate its symbolical meaning, and also to remind us that it was the standard of the Vikings. It was ' a blot in heaven,' not only because it showed black against the sky, but also because of the suggestion of fields of slaughter which it conveyed, darkening thus the daylight to the senses of the conscience-striken queen. "The Raven, the sacred bird of Odin, the Northern War-God, has always been deemed a bird of evil augury " (Littledale, *Essays*, etc., p. 280).

133. **Croak'd.** Observe the force of the word in this position : Cf. *Lancelot and Elaine*, 456,

> " Meet in the midst and there so furiously
> Shock, that a man," etc.

Holy Grail, 495,

> " The lightnings here and there to left and right
> Struck."

In fact this pause after a monosyllable at the beginning of a line is one of Tennyson's favourite rhythmical effects: cp. *Gareth and Lynette*, 305; *Holy Grail*, 82, 110, etc.

134. the Heathen of the Northern Sea, that is, the Angles and Saxons, swarming overseas, from whose invasions Arthur had delivered the land for a time.

135. Lured by the crimes, etc., that is, tempted by the weakness of which the debasement of morals gives promise. The queen's imagination naturally exaggerates the immediate effects of the catastrophe. A 'lure' is properly a piece of meat used to induce a hawk to return to the falconer. "A term of the chase, and therefore of French origin" (Skeat, *Etym. Dict.*).

140. yield, 'give.'

sanctuary is here not the inviolable asylum itself, but the protection which it affords.

141. Her name to whom, 'the name of her to whom.'

142. power, that is, the power of personal influence which they felt in her character.

143. Wrought, 'worked,' the strong form of the past tense.

147. housel is the Sacrament of the Lord's Supper. The original meaning of the word is 'sacrifice,' derived from a root meaning to kill. We have also the verb 'to housel' meaning to administer this Sacrament to a person, and 'to be houselled,' meaning to receive it: cp. Shakspeare, *Hamlet*, I. v. 73,

"Unhousel'd, disappointed, unanel'd."

Spenser (*Faerie Queene*, I. xii. 37) uses the word 'housling' in a more general sense: there "the housling fire" is "the sacramental fire" symbolical of marriage.

shrift, that is, confession, or absolution after confession; 'to shrive' is properly to impose penance, hence to hear a confession. It seems to have been taken at a very early period from the Latin *scribere*, with the meaning to 'prescribe' a penalty (Skeat. *Etym. Dict.*).

148. the little maid, see l. 3.

149. babbling heedlessness, that is, carelessness in speech, which led her to babble on like a brook without much thinking what she said.

150. lured her from herself, *i.e.* insensibly drew her away from thoughts of herself and of the evil work that she had done.

151. This night, see ll. 1-8; it is the point of time at which the idyll begins.

wildly blown about, a natural metaphor, the wind which carries things hither and thither being a fit representative of the force which spreads rumour abroad.

153. **him**, that is 'himself,' frequent in older English ; *e.g.* Shakspeare, *Rom.* I. v. 68,

"He bears him like a portly gentleman ";

1 *Henry IV.*, III. ii. 180,

"Advantage feeds him fat while men delay."

So also 'me,' 'thee,' 'her,' etc., for 'myself,' 'thyself,' 'herself,' etc.

157. **brook'd,** 'endured.' The word is from the Old English 'brucan,' to enjoy, which came to be used especially of food, hence in the fifteenth century 'to brook' is to digest, as, "He hath eaten raw quayles, I fear me he shall never be able to brooke them." From this we get naturally enough the meaning to endure or put up with, generally with a negative.

158. **brake it,** *i.e.* brake the silence.

160. **by and by** means originally 'in order,' 'one after another,' then 'immediately after,' 'straightway,' as in the Gospel of *St. Luke*, xxi. 9, "the end is not by and by." Finally this meaning is extended, like that of 'presently,' into the sense of 'after a time' (*New Engl. Dict.*).

163. **ye list,** 'you desire'; the verb is usually impersonal in older English, and Chaucer says "if thee list "; but it is not so in Shakspeare, *e.g.* "take 't as thou list " (*Tempest*, III. ii. 136), and "I list not prophecy " (*Winter's Tale*, IV. i. 26).

164. **unbind my heart.** The queen's trouble has numbed her heart, so that her feeling cannot find its proper outlet. Her tears are frozen, as it were, at their fountain, and she must be moved by some other emotion before they can flow and relieve her bursting heart.

165. **Whereat full willingly sang,** etc. Note the effect of the rhythm.

166. **Late, late, so late,** etc. The subject of the song is of course taken from the parable of the Ten Virgins (*Gospel of St. Matthew*, xxv. 1-13). Those who have no oil in their vessels have gone to get it from "them that sell," and in the meantime the bridegroom has returned from his procession through the streets of the town, the rest have gone in with him to the house, and the doors have been shut. They appeal for admittance acknowledging their neglect, but are answered sternly with the sentence,

"Too late, too late, ye cannot enter now."

The repetition of this burden chiming with the "Late, late, so late ! " which sets the keynote of the song, gives great intensity to this lyric.

180. Her thought when first she came is that recorded in l. 130,
"And in herself she moaned, 'Too late, too late!'"

183. let my words; the verb is in l. 186, "Comfort your
sorrows."

184. knows but to obey, 'knows only how to obey': 'but,'
which originally means 'except,' has now come to mean the same
as 'nothing but.' For example in *Gareth and Lynette* we have
"I mock thee not but as thou mockest me" (l. 283), where it
follows a negative, and also, "But to be won by force" (l. 104),
and "whom they could but love" (l. 681).

189. weigh your sorrows with, *i.e.* compare them with.

191. grim, 'fierce'; see note on l. 69.

192. Tennyson represents that though the queen had refused
Lancelot's proposal (l. 110 ff.), it was popularly supposed that she
was held by Lancelot in the castle overseas against which
Arthur was warring, her flight to Almesbury having been
unknown to all except herself and Lancelot. The situation in
fact is something like that which we find in one version of the
tale of Troy, which represents that Helen, who was supposed to
be in the besieged city, was really living in Egypt, and was
represented at Troy by a phantom.

193. And Modred, etc. She breaks off, leaving the sentence
unfinished; 'hath usurped the realm' is what she would have
said (see l. 152).

196. thrice as great, because of the threefold aspect of it which
she had named. The griefs of common folk touch themselves
alone.

as any of ours: the hurried rhythm gives some additional
energy to the assertion; so in the *Holy Grail*, 247:

"Broader and higher than any in all the lands."

198. come, notice the subjunctive.

205. The rather abrupt pause after the first word of the line is
intended to emphasize, and also in some degree rhythmically to
represent, the object of the desire.

behind a cloud, that is, in secret.

211. For the rhythm compare l. 70.

216. this is all woman's grief, that is, it is not only with the
common grief of all the realm that we women ought to grieve,
but with a special sorrow for ourselves, because she is woman
who hath wrought this evil.

222. Then thought the Queen, etc. For the repetition from
l. 211 ff. see note on l. 125.

223. prate, 'idle talk.' The frequentative form is 'prattle.'

225. The word 'nunnery,' for convent, has something of a contemptuous meaning. The time has not yet quite come when the queen will desire for herself too no other lot than to be shut within these nunnery walls of which she speaks.

229. Note the hurried rhythm at the end of the line; cp. ll. 181 and 274.

234. **Lyonnesse,** in the geography of the *Morte Darthur*, is a country to the south-west of Britain, apparently conceived as a continuation of Cornwall towards the Scilly Isles. The father of Tristram was king of it, and he is called Sir Tristram of Lyones. In the *Morte Darthur* he rides from Lyones into Cornwall, therefore it is evidently not conceived as over sea.

239. **Each,** that is, each headland. They are spoken of almost as living persons, the whole land being "full of life." The "wild sea-light" is the gleam of the stormy surf. Note the picturesqueness of the description.

242. **the rich heart of the west.** The western sky is to be conceived as still lighted with the after-glow of sunset.

244. **man-breasted things :** creatures partly in human and partly in animal form, represented here as rising from the sea and bellowing.

246. **the little elves.** Elves are originally, perhaps, spirits of the mountain, and that meaning would suit this passage well enough : but probably no distinction is intended between them and the fairies in general, those spirits of the forest, field and hill, of which Chaucer speaks in the *Canterbury Tales,* as having been banished from this England of ours by the begging friars :

> " In tholde dayes of the king Arthour,
> Of which that Britons speken greet honour,
> All was this land fulfild of fayerye.
> The elf-queen, with hir joly companye,
> Danced ful ofte in many a grene mede ;
> This was the olde opinion, as I rede.
> I speke of manye hundred yeres ago ;
> But now can no man see none elves mo.
> For now the grete charitee and prayeres
> Of limitours and othere holy freres,
> That serchen every lond and every streem,
> As thikke as motes in the sonne-beem,
> Blessinge halles, chambres, kitchenes, boures,
>
> .   .   .   .   .   .
>
> This maketh that ther been no fayeryes.
> For ther as wont to walken was an elf,
> There walketh now the limitour him-self," etc.
> — *Wyf of Bathes Tale,* 1 ff.

The description is a humorous one, but it expresses a genuine popular tradition, namely, that in 'the olden days,' and especially in the days of King Arthur, the land of Britain was full of elves and fairies, which have since in a great measure deserted it.

247. sounding like a distant horn : cf. *Princess*, IV. 9 :

> " O sweet and far from cliff and scar
> The horns of Elfland faintly blowing ! "

252. as the thistle shakes, etc.   Note the picturesque quality of Tennyson's similes and the accuracy of his observation. Other examples of similes drawn from bird life are—*Marriage of Geraint*, 774 :

> " As careful robins eye the delver's toil " ;

Lancelot and Elaine, 889 ff. :

> " Then as a little helpless, innocent bird,
> That has but one plain passage of few notes,
> Will sing the simple passage o'er and o'er
> For all an April morning, till the ear
> Wearies to hear it, so the simple maid," etc.

254. still, ' ever ': the usual meaning in older English and often in Tennyson, *e.g. Lady of Shalott*, 64 :

> " But in her web she still delights
> To weave the mirror's magic sights " ;

Gareth and Lynette, 1218 :

> " Who being still rebuked, would answer still
> Courteous as any knight."

255. flickering : a picturesque word, used also of the upward flight of the lark ; *Princess*, VII. 30 :

> " morn by morn the lark
> Shot up and shrill'd in flickering gyres."

Also of the motion of the lightning flash :

> "The livid-flickering fork " (*Merlin and Vivien*).

256. wheel'd and broke Flying. Note the exact repetition, here representing the repeated action ; this is to be distinguished from that repetition with variation which is often used for emphasis or with a pathetic effect.

260. swung round, a picturesque expression, representing the rhythmic whirl of the movement.

the lighted lantern of the hall is apparently the so-called lantern which forms a kind of sky-light in the roof of some college halls (*e.g.* that of Trinity College, Cambridge).   It is lighted in this case by the blaze of illumination within, and the wreath of airy dancers swing round it outside. This is clear not only on general grounds of probability, but also from the distinction between the outside and the inside of the hall, which we find marked in the next line, "And in the hall itself," etc.

263. Had whatsoever meat, etc. This in the Arthur romances is one of the phenomena which accompany the appearance of the Sangrail. For example in Malory's *Morte Darthur*, when the Grail passes through the hall, "every knight had such meats and drinks as he best loved in this world." This in the romances was the special characteristic of the court of king Pelles, where the Holy Grail was supposed to be kept.

Tennyson, wishing to spiritualize the Grail legend, has very happily brought in this incident in another connexion.

265. Down in the cellars, etc. For this Mr. Churton Collins refers to Croker's *Irish Fairy Legends*, p. 99 of the latest edition : "On advancing [he] perceived a little figure, about six inches in height, seated astride upon a pipe of the oldest port in the place, and bearing a spigot upon his shoulder."

266. the spigot is the stopper of the air-hole at the top of the cask, which would be removed to make the wine run freely.

275. a bard. This is the name given to the ancient Celtic poets, who constituted an established order among the people of Gaul and Britain, and had hereditary privileges. They were singers of patriotic and religious songs, such as those referred to in these lines. Merlin and Taliessin were bards.

276. Full many a noble war-song, etc. The bard is here represented as encouraging his people to resist the landing of the enemy from his fleet by war-songs chanted upon the shore between the cliff and the sea.

279. many a mystic lay. These are the religious songs praising God and speaking of the mysteries of human life.

280. smoky : that is, mist-covered.

281. The description is of an audience eagerly listening and moved with enthusiastic excitement. It is a fine imaginative picture.

283. that night, that is, on the night of that feast in Arthur's hall.

286. the false son of Gorloïs : that is, the base-born son of Gorloïs, reputed the son of Gorloïs but in fact a bastard. As to the question of Arthur's birth, see *Coming of Arthur*, 184-236. The story was that King Uther had loved Ygerne, the wife of Gorloïs, a Cornish prince, and, being repulsed by her, went to war with Gorloïs and slew him, and then, having captured Tintagil, enforced Ygerne "to wed him in her tears." Not

many months after this Uther died, and that same night a son was
born to Ygerne, who was delivered to Merlin to be brought up,
and at last was produced as Uther's heir. The other story,
which is here mentioned as told by the bard, is to be found in
the *Coming of Arthur*, ll. 358-410.

289. the thundering shores of Bude and Bos: that is, the
rocky north coast of Cornwall, upon which the long Atlantic
wave rolls and breaks in thunder. Note the rhythmical
quality of the line, in which the names are chosen so as to give
effect to the sound represented. Bude is a small harbour near
the northern limit of the county of Cornwall. Bos or Boscastle
is near Tintagil Head.

292. dark Tintagil: called "wild Dundagil" in the first
edition of the idyll. Tintagil Castle, of which the ruins exist
upon the north coast of Cornwall, was the reputed birth-place of
Arthur.

294. by miracle: that is, according to the romances, by the
power to draw a sword out of a stone, which all assayed to do
but none could achieve except Arthur (*Morte Darthur*, i. 3, 4).

approven, a more uncommon form, and therefore preferred by
Tennyson.

295. And that, etc. The whole of the story (ll. 287-299) is
reported indirectly as told by the bard.

296. and could he find, etc. Tennyson's own ideas about the
strength to be gained by perfect marriage are expressed in the
Princess, VII. 285 ff.:
> " each fulfils
> Defect in each, and always thought in thought,
> Purpose in purpose, will in will, they grow,
> The single pure and perfect animal,
> The two-celled heart beating, with one full stroke,
> Life."

302. reel'd, 'staggered.' This sense is apparently derived
from that of winding upon a reel, hence intrans. 'to turn round'
(Skeat, *Etym. Dict.*).

308. play upon me. The metaphor is perhaps, as in *Hamlet*,
from a musical instrument, the idea of touching the keys of an
instrument in order to test its sound. The queen thinks that
the Abbess and nuns, simple as they seem to be, have set this
little novice to find out who she is. The expression is also used
however in a different sense, as *Gareth and Lynette*, 1221 : "only
wondering wherefore play'd upon," where it means 'mocked.'

310. Note the hurried rhythm and effect produced by the
arrangement of words at the end of the line.

311. **gadding**, 'wandering,' with the idea of straying idly beyond bounds : so Milton speaks of ' the gadding vine.'

314. **Unmannerly**, used as adverb, having already the adverbial termination '-ly': so with other adjectives of the same form, as ' friendly,' ' womanly,' etc., especially in poetry; *e.g. Lancelot and Elaine*, 236 : " Full courtly and not falsely thus returned "; and l. 39 of this idyll.

319. **come next**, that is, ' come next summer ': as we might say, ' three years ago, come Martinmas.' She means that next summer it will be five years since his death.

323. **But pray you.** The word ' but ' resumes the speech after the break of the line before ; so in Latin *sed* or *autem* might be used, and in Greek δέ. The imitation of these classical usages is rather characteristic of Tennyson; cf. the use of ' for ' in such expressions as, "Yet ... for ye know," etc., *Holy Grail*, 315 and elsewhere.

327. **the same**, *i.e.* ' so also,' like Latin *idem*.

329. **Forbore his own advantage** : that is, abstained from pushing the advantage he might have gained over his adversary to the uttermost point. Compare the account given by Arthur of Lancelot's manners in fight, *Lancelot and Elaine*, ll. 1346-1353 :

> " for I know
> What thou hast been in battle by my side,
> And many a time have watched thee at the tilt
> Strike down the lusty and long practised knight,
> And let the younger and unskilled go by
> To win his honour and to make his name,
> And loved thy courtesies and thee, a man
> Made to be loved."

333. **manners are not idle**, that is, they are not a mere outward show, without significance, but grow out the nature of the man. The importance attached to ' manners ' was a characteristic of the age of chivalry. Tennyson takes care to point out that manners must not consist in a mere superficial courtesy. Gawain, who is called the Courteous, is the type in the *Idylls* of the man who may have a smile on his face but a frown on his heart, and he, while claiming credit for his courtesy to Elaine, is rebuked by the king for lack of the higher courtesy which should have been shown in obedience to the commands laid upon him.

335. **such fair fruit**, *i.e.* fruit of such a fair tree.

337. **as all rumour runs**, ' as fame currently reports.'

340. **O closed about**, etc.   Cf. l. 225.

342. **all the wealth and all the woe**, that is, all the weal and all the woe, ' wealth ' used here as in older English.

345. the doom of fire refers doubtless to the fire of purgatory, that by which the soul of Hamlet's father was tormented :

" Doom'd for a certain time to walk the night
And, for the day, confin'd to fast in fires,
Till the foul crimes, done in my days of nature
Are burnt and purged away."—*Hamlet*, I. v. 9.

The fire of eternal damnation is too shocking a doom to be imagined by the queen for Lancelot as a punishment for so slight an offence as she here describes :

" If ever Lancelot, that most noble knight,
Were for one hour less noble than himself."

348. his, *i.e.* his manners.

353. Whom she would soothe, *i.e.* ' her whom she desired to soothe ': for the omission of the pronoun cf. *Gareth and Lynette*, 548, " make demand of whom ye gave me to "; also 680, 681.

358. harry, properly means to make war upon, or devastate by war.

360. aghast, see note on l. 78. This word is a past participle from the Old English ' agasten,' to terrify, unless it be rather from some collateral form like *agasen*, such as seems to be implied by the form ' agaste ' for the past tense in Chaucer.

362. As tremulously, etc. The picturesqueness of the simile is made still more effective by the rhythm. It is another instance of the poet's accurate observation of things in nature.

371. but in thought—Not ev'n in inmost thought, etc. The form of the expression is changed after the pause. She might have said, ' What is true repentance but in thought to abandon the sin.' The change to a negative form makes the renunciation more emphatic, while at the same time a certain tenderness is brought into it which leads to the slipping back into thoughts of the past and becoming again half-guilty.

375. To see him more : a musing repetition, while she passes to thoughts of the time when she saw him first.

377. the golden days : cf. *Recollections of the Arabian Nights*:

" In sooth it was a goodly time,
For it was in the golden prime
Of good Haroun Alraschid."

378. when Lancelot came, etc. See *Coming of Arthur*, 446-451 :

" Then Arthur charged his warrior whom he loved
And honour'd most, Sir Lancelot, to ride forth
And bring the Queen ;—and watch'd him from the gates :
And Lancelot past away among the flowers,

(For then was latter April) and return'd
Among the flowers, in May, with Guinevere."

And also the graceful fragment, *Sir Lancelot and Queen Guinevere*.

383. **Rapt,** 'carried away,' hence of an emotion or occupation which absorbs the whole attention: cf. *Marriage of Geraint*, 529:

" Rapt in the fear and in the wonder of it."

Milton, *Paradise Lost*, iii. 522, has it in the literal sense :

" Rapt in a chariot drawn by fiery steeds."

The word is of English origin, from ' rap,' ' snatch,' but it has been supposed to come from the Latin *rapere*.

384. **the time Was maytime,** etc. The season suggested such talk of love and of pleasure, and there was as yet no consciousness of guilt to make their talk less free.

388. **That seem'd the heavens,** etc. The thought would be suggested by the pure and intense blue of the flower and the manner in which the whole ground was covered by the sheets of blossom. Cf. Chaucer, *Book of the Duchesse*, 388 f.,

" As thogh the erthe envye wolde
To be gayer than the heven."

Mr. Littledale remarks, " In the villages of the inner Himalayas a like beautiful appearance is visible in May, but is there caused by the forget-me-nots that cover the mountain-meadows till they seem ' a little sky Gulf'd in a world below ' " (*Essays on the Idylls*, p. 284).

395. **The Dragon,** etc. This was the symbol of royalty among the Britons, and stands for the sign of Arthur's lordship over the other kings and chiefs of the land. The title Pendragon (*i.e.* Dragon's head) is said to have been taken by Uther in consequence of an appearance which he saw in the sky (Geoffrey of Monmouth, *Hist. Brit*, 8, 14-17). The Pendragonship therefore is this superior sovereignty supposed to have been exercised first by Uther and then by Arthur, who is called "The dread Pendragon, Britain's King of kings." In the *Idylls* Arthur bears the golden dragon as crest, and it appears generally as his symbol : see *Lancelot and Elaine*, 426 ff. :

'' easily to be known,
Since to his crown the golden dragon clung
And down his robe the dragon writhed in gold,
And from the carven-work behind him crept
Two dragons gilded, sloping down to make
Arms for his chair, while all the rest of them
Thro' knots and loops and folds innumerable
Fled ever thro' the woodwork."

In this idyll, 590 ff., we hear of the golden dragon as the crest

of Arthur's helmet, and in l. 594 the line which we have here
is repeated with reference to it.   Here it is the device on the
royal banner which floats over the pavilions set up for the queen.

396. **the state pavilion of the King** is in this instance that
which he has ordered to be prepared for her reception at each
halt.   The word ' pavilion ' comes through French from the
Latin *papilio*, ' butterfly,' and means originally a wide-spread
tent of brilliant colours.

398. **trance** is originally from the Latin *transitus*, a state of
transition or suspense, hence used of reflections which suspend
consciousness of the present.

402. **thought him cold**, etc.   The feeling of the queen about
Arthur is clearly expressed in *Lancelot and Elaine*, 120 ff. :

> " Arthur, my lord, Arthur, the faultless King,
>   That passionate perfection, my good lord—
>   But who can gaze upon the Sun in heaven ?
> .   .   .   .
> .   .   .   .   but, friend, to me
>   He is all fault who hath no fault at all :
>   For who loves me must have a touch of earth ;
>   The low sun makes the colour."

403. **passionless.**   The word is equivalent to a dissyllable in
the verse.   In the succeeding lines a good many instances occur
of words like ' murmuring,' ' listening,' ' gallery,' ' shadowy,'
etc., slurred in a similar manner.

408. **Then on a sudden a cry :** note the rhythm, giving the
effect of a startling sound.

411. **Rang coming.**   A monosyllable at the beginning of the
line, followed by a pause, is often used by Tennyson to express
sudden action or sound : cf. note on l. 107.   Here the more con-
tinuous sound of armed feet approaching along the gallery is
expressed by the less abrupt pause after the second word.   Compare the rhythm of l. 416, where the sound ceases.

prone, ' forwards,' from Latin *pronus*.

412. **grovell'd**, ' lay face downwards.' In older English we
have the adverbs ' grof ' or ' groveling ' to express this position,
and hence comes the verb ' to grovel.'

417. **like a Ghost's Denouncing judgment :** like the voice of a
spirit from the dead threatening punishment to the living who
have done it wrong.

419. **of one I honour'd**, etc.   That is, of Leodogran, king of
Cameliard, who is happy, says Arthur, because he has not lived
to see his daughter's shame.

421. **Well is it, etc.** The passage is easy from the thought of the father, on whom shame had been brought by his daughter, to the idea of children to whom their mother's shame would have descended. Then the mention of children leads to the thought of the progeny of evils to which Guinevere's sin has given birth.

423. **Red ruin:** a forcible expression, both because of its alliteration and its picturesqueness.

424. **the craft of kindred** refers to the treachery of Modred, Arthur's supposed nephew, who has leagued himself with the Saxons and raised revolt against Arthur.

429. **In twelve great battles.** These are all enumerated (from Nennius) in *Lancelot and Elaine*, 284 ff. :

> "And Lancelot spoke
> And answer'd him at full, as having been
> With Arthur in the fight which all day long
> Rang by the white mouth of the violent Glem ;
> And in the four loud battles by the shore
> Of Duglas ; that on Bassa ; then the war
> That thunder'd in and out the gloomy skirts
> Of Celidon the forest ; and again
> By castle Gurnion, where the glorious King
> Had on his cuirass worn our Lady's Head,
> Carved of one emerald center'd in a sun
> Of silver rays, that lighten'd as he breath'd ;
> And at Caerleon had he help'd his lord,
> When the strong neighings of the wild white Horse
> Set every gilded parapet shuddering ;
> And up in Agned-Cathregonion too,
> And down the waste sand-shores of Trath-Treroit,
> Where many a heathen fell ; 'and on the mount
> Of Badon I myself beheld the King
> Charge at the head of all his Table Round,' " etc.

ruining: 'hurling down': a fine word, which Tennyson uses elsewhere in the sense of rushing down headlong, *Lucretius*, 40:

"Ruining along the illimitable inane."

Both senses are connected with the uses of the Latin *ruere*.

433. **Had yet that grace of courtesy, etc.** Cf. *Morte Darthur*, xx. 13, where it is related how in the fighting about Lancelot's castle of Joyous Gard, Lancelot forbore the person of the king, and when Arthur was unhorsed and Sir Bors would have slain him, " Not so hardy, said Sir Launcelot, upon pain of thy head that thou touch him no more ; for I will never see that most

noble king that made me knight, neither slain ne shamed." The construction is:

"Had yet so much courtesy left that he spared," etc.

436. all his kith and kin. The devotion of Lancelot's kinsmen to him is well marked in the romances and also by Tennyson in the *Idylls*, *e.g. Holy Grail*, 648 :

"For Lancelot's kith and kin so worship him
That ill to him is ill to them."

See also *Lancelot and Elaine*, 464 ff.

kith is connected with words meaning to know or make known, as 'ken,' 'kythe,' etc. It is hardly used in modern English except in this expression 'kith and kin,' meaning relations and connexions.

439. troth and fealty, 'truth and fidelity,' that is, loyalty to their king, with special reference to the oath of homage and fealty.

444. but a hair, 'only a hair,' that is, 'even so much as a hair.'

451. Bear with me, etc. Objections have been raised to the fine passage which follows, on the ground that it argues some want of generosity in the king thus to press home his wife's misdoing and the injury inflicted upon himself, when she was lying crushed and humiliated at his feet. It must be admitted that there is some force in this criticism, but it may be remembered, on the other hand, first, that the theme is heroic, and all private considerations may fairly be made to give way before the greatness of the issues involved ; and, secondly, that it is in part for her sake that he thus enforces the wrong. His duty to her compels him to make her feel the full extent of the evil which her sin has wrought and to bring home to her the fact that, though he still loved her, it was impossible that she should ever return to him as his wife, impossible if he had been merely in a private station, and most of all impossible since he is the king. To set her mind at rest on that point, and to persuade her that they might yet meet again as husband and wife in another world, if she would labour to purify her soul in this, was the highest and truest proof of love that he could give ; and the appeal to her to leave him at least the hope of meeting her again, gives a touch of healing grace to the bitterness of enforced separation.

455. here and there a deed, etc. These are the deeds of that 'knighthood-errant' which Arthur first drew together and made effective. His dislike of random adventures is brought out in the *Holy Grail, e.g.* 272 ff. :   "his face
Darken'd, as I have seen it more than once,
When some brave deed seem'd to be done in vain,
Darken."

456. a random wrong is here a wrong done in a casual and disorderly manner. The Old French *randon* means the force or swiftness of a stream, hence careless haste or impetuosity.

457. But I was first, etc. Compare the opening passage of the *Idylls*:

> " For many a petty king ere Arthur came
> Ruled in this isle, and ever waging war
> Each upon other, wasted all the land :
> And still from time to time the heathen host
> Swarm'd overseas, and harried what was left.
> And so there grew great tracts of wilderness,
> Wherein the beast was ever more and more,
> But man was less and less, till Arthur came.
> For first Aurelius lived and fought and died,
> And after him King Uther fought and died,
> But either failed to make the kingdom one.
> And after these King Arthur for a space,
> And thro' the puissance of his Table Round,
> Drew all their petty princedoms under him,
> Their king and head, and made a realm, and reign'd."
> *Coming of Arthur*, 5-19.

458. the knighthood-errant : the body of knights-errant, that is, of those who wandered abroad aimlessly in search of adventures.

this realm and all The realms would be the realm of Logris or England (as it is often called in the romances), with the other kingdoms in and about Britain, viz., Cameliard, Cornwall, North Wales, Gore, Northumberland, Scotland, Orkney, Ireland, and others.

460-480. This is the classic passage in the *Idylls* for the Table Round and the oath sworn by the knights of it, and it seems to express Tennyson's ideal of chivalry, a much higher one than any which we find in the romances.

462. model for the mighty world. The Round Table is said in some of the romances to have been made by Merlin as an emblem of the round world. Here, however, the meaning is that it was to be an example for the world to imitate.

464. lay their hands in mine : the form observed in doing feudal homage.

467. the Christ, as a title, meaning 'the Anointed,' corresponding to the Hebrew ' Messiah.'

470. his own word. Note the change to the singular, which is more suitable for what follows :

" To love one maiden only," etc.

D

475. subtle, not so much crafty or skilful, as all-penetrating, insensibly pervading the whole nature : the word means originally thin or delicate.

476. maiden passion, that is, passion of first love (or perhaps of pure love). This doctrine of love is here nearly the same as the mediæval ideal, in which love takes the place of religion; but reverence for God and loyalty to the king are here combined with it in the institution of the perfect knight. In the romances of chivalry love stands almost alone as the source of all that is honourable and praiseworthy.

482. Believing, "lo mine helpmate," etc. Cf. *Coming of Arthur*, 89-93 :

> " But were I joined with her,
> Then might we live together as one life,
> And reigning with one will in everything
> Have power on this dark land to lighten it,
> And power on this dead world to make it live."

helpmate. The word is apparently due originally to a mistaken notion of the phrase "an help meet for him," in *Genesis*, ii. 18, 20, and has been used for 'helper' with reference especially to the relation of man and wife.

485. the sin of Tristram and Isolt. For this see the *Last Tournament*. The story is one of the most famous of the Arthurian cycle, but originally does not belong to it and is not at all essential to its development. Tennyson's Tristram professes that he has taken the vows to Arthur in a moment of exaltation, and that he knows them to be impossible to keep. Isolt was the daughter of King Anguish of Ireland, and Tristram, bringing her over as bride for his uncle Mark, king of Cornwall, had drunk with her a love-potion which compelled them ever afterwards to love one another. He married another Isolt of Brittany, called "Isolt les blanches mains," but he was irresistibly drawn back by the remembrance of his former love, "la Belle Isolt," and at last was killed treacherously by Mark, her husband, while harping before her.

> "'Mark's way,' said Mark, and clove him thro' the brain."

487. The fair names naturally made the ill example more dangerous.

489. destined, 'intended.'

obtain, 'prevail,' like Latin *obtinere*.

491. He means that he now guards his life as a duty and because it is God's gift, not because he denies to preserve it for his own sake.

scathe, ' harm,' from the verb ' to scathe,' *e.g.* :

"This truth may chance to scathe you"

(Shakspeare, *Rom.* i. v. 86).

From it we have the adjective 'scatheless.'

492. think, *i.e.* 'I think.'

495. my knights : rather a bold change from the third person to the first: cf. l. 470, where the change is from plural to singular.

497. Cf. l. 377.

499. glance at, *i.e.* refer to with censure, because of her want of purity.

500. bowers, *i.e.* chambers.

Camelot is the place where Arthur chiefly holds his court. Caxton, in his preface to Malory's *Morte Darthur*, speaks of it as if it were in Wales, probably confusing it with Caerleon, but Malory himself identifies it with Winchester. There was, however, a Camelot or Camelat in Somersetshire, represented now by the villages of East and West Camel, which have the remains of an ancient town and are said to be full of Arthurian traditions. In Tennyson's *Idylls* Camelot is a mystic city, the locality of which the poet does not attempt to fix precisely. It is described more especially in *Gareth and Lynette*, 184-193, 296-302, and *Holy Grail*, 225-257, 339-360.

Usk here stands for Caerleon-upon-Usk, the Roman town of Isca Silurum, in Monmouthshire, on the river Usk above Newport. In romance it is one of the principal residences of Arthur, and the Roman amphitheatre there is called Arthur's Round Table. The idylls of the *Marriage of Geraint* and *Pelleas and Ettarre* have their scenes partly laid there.

501 ff. With these lines should be compared the passage of Æschylus, where the desolation of the house of Menelaus after the flight of Helen is described :—

Ἰὼ, ἰὼ δῶμα, δῶμα καὶ πρόμοι,
Ἰὼ λέχος καὶ στίβοι φιλάνορες.
Πάρεστι σιγᾶς, ἄτιμος, ἀλοίδορος,
Ἄδιστος ἀφεμένων ἰδεῖν.
Πόθῳ δ' ὑπερποντίας
Φάσμα δόξει δόμων ἀνάσσειν.—*Agam.* 419-424.

Thus translated by Plumptre :—

" Woe for that kingly house and for its chiefs !
Woe for the marriage bed and traces left
    Of wife who loved her lord !
There stands he silent ; foully wronged, and yet
    Uttering no word of scorn,

> In deepest woe perceiving she is gone ;
>   And in his yearning love
>   For one beyond the sea
>   A ghost shall seem to queen it o'er his house."

503. vacant ornament, that is, ornament no longer worn by thee.

507. of so slight elements, that is, of materials so slight as to be easily unmade and made again in a different fashion.

509. I hold that man, etc. The passage has a rather rhetorical and sententious character, which recalls the style of the Greek dramatists, especially Euripides.

511. his blood, that is, his family and descendants, who would share in the dishonour of the unfaithful wife and mother.

scandal is public reproach and dishonour (more properly that which causes reproach or offence), from Gr. σκάνδαλον, a snare or a stumbling-block.

The reference to the case of those who had children that might suffer from the scandal may be taken to be an additional enforcement of the rule in the case of those who had none. If the erring wife must not be restored to her place even to save the children from shame, then still less where there existed no such motive.

514. Her station, i.e. her position as an honourable wife.

515. a new disease, unknown to men. The danger lies in the fact that the evil is unrecognized, its symptoms are either unknown or concealed. She is like one infected with a deadly disease, but supposed to be healthy, and therefore allowed to move everywhere among the crowd without precaution. Simile and metaphor are here combined. She is said to be "like a new disease," and then she is identified with it, and

> "Creeps, no precaution used, among the crowd."

517. saps The fealty of our friends, because they are half-unwittingly drawn into a relation with her which is doubtfully loyal to the husband.

520. Worst of the worst, that is, 'worst of the worst public foes,' an additional emphasis on the expression in l. 509.

523. mockery, because the fact of seeing her reseated in her place would seem to them a mockery of their sense of right.

bane, 'destruction,' connected with words meaning to strike or slay. In English the word has come to mean especially poison ; cp. 'ratsbane,' 'henbane,' etc.

524. He paused. Mr. Elsdale remarks that this pause is artistically very advantageous, as breaking the sustained monotony of the king's speech (Studies in the Idylls, p. 102).

526. Far off a solitary trumpet blew. The effect of this far off sound breaking the silence of the pause, and answered by the nearer neigh of the war horse at the door, is very striking, and makes the solemnity of the silence more impressive.

Mr. Elsdale remarks: "Arthur has said his say and unburdened his soul. He has unfolded, not without a noble indignation, the spoilt purpose of his life and the sin which she has sinned. And now the trumpet calls him to his unknown fate, and the expectant neigh of his faithful steed, who recognizes the martial summons and enquires loudly for his master, reminds him that his time is short. Is there no place for that vast pity which fills him and for the love which has wrought into his very life? To that pity and that love the imploring action of his poor prostrate Queen, mutely protesting against the extreme severity of his last words, makes a silent appeal. Accordingly he begins again in a changed tone. Instead of an utterance of righteous indignation, we have now one full of loving forgiveness and sorrowful farewell" (*Studies in the Idylls*, p. 102).

534. The wrath which, etc. In the *Morte Darthur* Guinevere was condemned to the fire by Arthur, and only rescued by Lancelot when actually brought to the stake. In fact she had been frequently before condemned to the same punishment: "Oftimes," says Lancelot, "ye have consented that she should be burnt and destroyed in your heat, and then it fortuned me to do battle for her" (*Morte Darthur*, xx. 11). It was necessary for the poet to modify this unchivalrous barbarity, and he has done so very happily without altogether dispensing with the circumstance, by representing it as a decision taken in a flash of momentary anger and speedily retracted.

535. The doom of treason: because in the queen adultery would be an act of treason; so at least it was held by English law in later times.

537. weigh'd thy heart with one, etc. *i.e.* compared thy heart with mine: cf. l. 189,

> "But weigh your sorrows with our lord the King's
> And weighing find them less."

543. But how to take, etc. Again we are reminded of the Greek dramatists, this time by the stateliness of the pathos and the suggestion of subtle irony.

554. For I was ever virgin, etc. This belongs to what follows: "Since thou wert the object of my only love, the love for thee hath so inter-penetrated my life that I cannot cast it away, and this is now the punishment for my over-great trust."

557. For the repetition, with some variation of the preceding line, cf. *Geraint and Enid*, 135 :

" I needs must disobey him for his good :
How should I dare obey him for his harm. '
It has the effect both of emphasis and pathos.   The queen her-
self repeats the same words in the same form afterwards, l. 668.

558. **so,** *i.e.* provided that, ' purify ' and ' lean ' being of
course subjunctives.

559. **our fair father Christ** : so in the *Coming of Arthur*, 509,
   " And we that fight for our fair father Christ."

564. **Nor Lancelot, nor another,** ' neither Lancelot nor any
other,' a phrase which the queen reproduces afterwards twice in
nearly the same words, ll. 645, 656.

570. **no kin of mine.**   Here Arthur is made to pronounce
decisively not only against the rumour which made Modred his
son, but also in favour of that mysterious and supernatural
origin for himself which is suggested in the *Coming of Arthur*,
358-410.   The first edition of *Guinevere* makes Modred the
nephew of Arthur, see note on l. 10.   The passage here ran
originally :
   " Where I must strike against my sister's son
   Leagued with the Lords of the White Horse and knights
   Once mine, and strike him dead."

571. **Lords of the White Horse,** see note on l. 15.

573. **Death, or I know not what,** etc.   Cf. *Coming of Arthur*,
418 ff :
                  " and Merlin in our time
   Hath spoken also, not in jest, and sworn
   Tho' men may wound him that he will not die,
   But pass, again to come."

576. **see thee no more.**   Unconsciously he echoes the vow
which the queen herself has made about Lancelot, see l. 374.

582. **found The casement.**   It seems to be implied that she
reached it with difficulty, being dazed in her anguish.

casement, properly the frame of a window, connected with
' case,' ' encase,' etc.   Here simply the window.

584. **If I might** : expressing a wish, as we commonly say ' if
only ' : so in Latin *e.g.* " Si nunc se nobis ille aureus arbore
ramus Ostendat " (Virg. *Aen.* vi. 187).

590-594. See note on l. 395.

592. **Which then was as an angel's** : cf. *Acts of the Apostles*, v.
15, " And all that sat in the council ... saw his face as it had
been the face of an angel."

594. Mr. Littledale quotes Spenser, *F. Q.* i. vii. 31, where
Arthur's crest is thus described :

"For all the crest a Dragon did enfold
    With greedy pawes, and over all did spredd
    His golden winges : his dreadful hideous hedd,
    Close couched on the bever, seem'd to throw
    From flaming mouth bright sparckles fiery redd,
    That sudden horrour to faint hartes did show ;
    And scaly tayle was stretcht adowne his back full low."

595. **Blaze, making all the night, etc.** Observe the emphatic position of the word 'Blaze': cf. *Holy Grail*, 108 ff:

"I heard a sound
As of a silver horn from o'er the hills
Blown."

The mist is described as lighted up all round with the blaze of the golden crest reflecting the flames of the torches.

598. The well-known effect of mist in increasing the size of figures by making them seem further away than they really are is here finely used by the poet to enhance the mystic grandeur of the scene.

604. **Then—as a stream, etc.** The reference is to some such fall as that of the Staubbach, in which the water disperses itself in spray during its passage through the air, but gathers again into a stream at the bottom.

606. **flashes down the vale**; cf. *In Memoriam*, XCVIII. :

"The cataract flashing from the bridge."

It is one of those picturesque words which Tennyson uses so effectively.

607. The hurried rhythm of the line with a sudden break before the fourth accent gives the effect of intensity to the speech.

611. **His mercy choked me.** She values his forgiveness, as we see from ll. 629, 659, etc., and means only that the emotions which she experienced in receiving it deprived her of the power of replying.   If the expression stood alone we might be inclined to understand it as expressing a passionate rejection of such forgiveness as she had received, given not from the common level of humanity, but from a divine height above it.

613. **of another**, that is, of Lancelot.

617. **If soul be soul**, that is if soul be immortal ; for the sin will still survive with it, though the body die.

623. **that defeat of fame**, *i.e.* that loss (or destruction) of good name and repute : cf. Shakspeare, *Much Ado*, IV. i. 48:

"And made defeat of her virginity."

628. **mockery is the fume of little hearts**: mockery is, as it were, the smoke which rises from the smouldering fire of petty rancour and jealousy in the heart of a mean man.   We use the

same kind of metaphor when we speak of fretting and fuming, and 'fumish' (from the French *fumieu*) is used in older English for 'melancholy' or 'ill-tempered.'

631. live down sin. The shame before the world can never be lived down, but the sin may be purged from the soul by living aright.

634. as is the conscience of a saint, etc. The whole purpose of the *Idylls* is to shadow "Sense at war with Soul," see the. lines *To the Queen* at the conclusion. Arthur is here pictured by Guinevere as the representative of Soul, not so much warring upon Sense as controlling it by guidance. His influence over his knights is as that of the conscience of a good man over the conflicting impulses of his moral nature. In this figure it is the senses that are represented as warring on one another and being harmonized and combined in useful action by the Soul.

640 ff. I thought I could not breathe, etc. With this compare the passage of *Lancelot and Elaine* quoted in the note on l. 402. The comparison suggested in those lines is to the pure bright light of midday on the heights, as compared with the slanting rays of the setting sun in the lowlands, which are more richly coloured because of the earth-vapours through which they shine :

"The low sun makes the colour."

642. yearn'd for, 'longed for.'

649. it were, that is, 'it would be.'

655. needs must : 'needs' (*i.e.* of necessity) is an adverb formed on the analogy of the genitive case-ending '-es,' but not actually taken from any such genitive, for the Old English form is 'nede,' from an Anglo-Saxon genitive in '-e' (Skeat, *Etym. Dict.*).

657. vail, 'lower': so *The Last Tournament*, 150 :

"He look'd but once, and vail'd his eyes again."

The word is originally 'avail,' from French *avaler*.

658. The word 'suppliant' is slurred, so as to be equivalent to one syllable only.

659. Yea, little maid. She replies to the mute appeal for forgiveness from the novice who had unwittingly offended her.

665. O shut me round, etc. She no longer speaks with contempt of the nunnery-walls and their narrowing influence (cf. ll. 225 and 340), but asks to be enclosed within them herself as a refuge from the cries of "scorn," which come from the world outside them. At the same time it is not mere cowardice that moves her to seek for refuge from those voices ; she must save herself from utter self-scorn, because the king still loves her, and that can only be by retiring from the world into "the quiet life."

668. Cf. 1. 557.

673. not grieving at your joys : a variation of the form of expression, intended to suggest that, though she might not rejoice in their joys, being unworthy of any life but one of penitence, she would not cast a gloom over them by seeming to disapprove.

675. lie before, 'prostrate myself in adoration before.'

677. dole : properly, a small portion of anything, hence of food distributed to the poor. The word is a variant of ' deal.'

679. haler, more sound in spite of their sickness, as they are also more rich in spite of their poverty.

682. sombre, 'dark,' that is, overshadowed by the consequences of guilt : from the French *sombre*, corresponding to the Spanish *sombrio*, and derived probably from a supposed Latin word *sub-umbrare*, to shadow. Tennyson has it also in its more literal sense, *Dream of Fair Women* :

" Thridding the sombre boskage of the wood."

685. is it yet too late ? The thought which had come to her as she fled over the glimmering waste to Almesbury, and had been echoed by the heedless novice in her song, returns to her now as a question not altogether without hope, though mingled also with fear.

688. ministration, ' serviceable work.'

689. the high rank she had borne. This is a very subordinate motive in the poet's version, but with the romancers it was sufficient without any other : " She was ruler and abbess, as reason would " (*Morte Darthur*, xxi. 7.).

691. an Abbess. Note the repetition so characteristic of the poet.

692. ''The pathetic gentleness of the cadence in the last line ... is as exquisite as that in Milton's finest verse :

"And I shall shortly be with them that rest ' "

(Littledale, *Essays on the Idylls of the King*, p. 287).

INDEX TO THE NOTES.

(The references are to the lines.)

GLASGOW : PRINTED AT THE UNIVERSITY PRESS BY ROBERT MACLEHOSE AND CO.

MACMILLAN'S
ENGLISH CLASSICS:

A SERIES OF SELECTIONS FROM THE
WORKS OF THE GREAT ENGLISH WRITERS,

WITH INTRODUCTION AND NOTES.

The following Volumes, Globe 8vo, are ready or in preparation.

ADDISON—SELECTIONS FROM THE SPECTATOR. By K. DEIGHTON. 2s. 6d.

BACON—ESSAYS. By F. G. SELBY, M.A. 3s. ; sewed, 2s. 6d.
The *Schoolmaster*—"A handy and serviceable edition of a famous English classical work, one that can never lose its freshness and its truth."

—THE ADVANCEMENT OF LEARNING. By F. G. SELBY, M.A. Book I., 2s. ; Book II., 4s. 6d.

BURKE—REFLECTIONS ON THE FRENCH REVOLUTION. By F. G. SELBY, M.A. 5s.
Scotsman—"Contains many notes which will make the book valuable beyond the circle to which it is immediately addressed."
Schoolmaster—"A very good book whether for examination or for independent reading and study."
Glasgow Herald—"The book is remarkably well edited."

—SPEECH ON AMERICAN TAXATION ; SPEECH ON CONCILIATION WITH AMERICA ; LETTER TO THE SHERIFFS OF BRISTOL. By F. G. SELBY, M.A. 3s. 6d.

CAMPBELL—SELECTIONS. By W. T. WEBB, M.A. [*In preparation.*

COWPER—THE TASK, BOOK IV. By W. T. WEBB, M.A. Sewed, 1s.

—SELECT LETTERS. By W. T. WEBB, M.A. 2s. 6d.

DRYDEN—SELECT SATIRES ; ABSALOM AND ACHITOPHEL ; THE MEDAL ; MACFLECKNOE. By J. CHURTON COLLINS, M.A. 1s. 9d.

GOLDSMITH—THE TRAVELLER and THE DESERTED VILLAGE. By ARTHUR BARRETT, B.A. 1s. 9d. THE TRAVELLER (separately), sewed, 1s. THE DESERTED VILLAGE (separately), sewed, 1s.
The *Scotsman*—"It has a short critical and biographical introduction, and a very full series of capital notes."

GRAY—POEMS. By JOHN BRADSHAW, LL.D. 1s. 9d.
Dublin Evening Mail—"The Introduction and Notes are all that can be desired. We believe that this will rightly become the standard school edition of Gray."
Schoolmaster—"One of the best school editions of Gray's poems we have seen."

MACMILLAN AND CO., LONDON.

HELPS—ESSAYS WRITTEN IN THE INTERVALS OF BUSINESS. By F. J. ROWE, M.A., and W. T. WEBB, M.A.   1s. 9d.
The *Literary World*—"These essays are, indeed, too good to be forgotten." The *Guardian*—"A welcome addition to our school classics. The introduction, though brief, is full of point."

JOHNSON—LIFE OF MILTON.   By K. DEIGHTON.   1s. 9d.

LAMB—ESSAYS OF ELIA.   By N. L. HALLWARD, M.A., and S. C. HILL, B.A.

MACAULAY—ESSAY ON LORD CLIVE.   By K. DEIGHTON.   2s.

—ESSAY ON WARREN HASTINGS.   By K. DEIGHTON.   2s. 6d.

—ESSAY ON ADDISON.   By Prof. J. W. HALES, M.A.   [*In the Press.*

MALORY—MORTE D'ARTHUR.   Edited by A. T. MARTIN.

MILTON—PARADISE LOST, BOOKS I. and II.   By MICHAEL MACMILLAN, B.A.   1s. 9d.   Books I. and II. separately, 1s. 3d. each ; sewed, 1s. each.
The *Times of India*—"The notes of course occupy the editor's chief attention, and form the most valuable part of the volume. They are clear, concise, and to the point, . . . while at the same time they are simple enough for the comprehension of students to whom Milton without annotation must needs be a mystery."
The *Schoolmaster*—"The volume is admirably adapted for use in upper classes of English Schools."
The *Educational News*—"For higher classes there can be no better book for reading, analysis, and grammar, and the issue of these books of Paradise Lost must be regarded as a great inducement to teachers to introduce higher literature into their classes."

—L'ALLEGRO, IL PENSEROSO, LYCIDAS, ARCADES, SONNETS, &c. By WILLIAM BELL, M.A.   1s. 9d.
The *Glasgow Herald*—"A careful study of this book will be as educative as that of any of our best critics on Aeschylus or Sophocles."

—COMUS.   By the same.   1s. 3d.; sewed, 1s.
The *Dublin Evening Mail*—"The introduction is well done, and contains much sound criticism."
The *Practical Teacher*—"The notes include everything a student could reasonably desire in the way of elucidations of the text, and at the same time are presented in so clear and distinct a fashion, that they are likely to attract the reader instead of repelling him."

—SAMSON AGONISTES.   By H. M. PERCIVAL, M.A.   2s.
The *Guardian*—"His notes are always of real literary value. . . . His introduction is equally masterly, and touches all that can be said about the poem."

SCOTT—THE LADY OF THE LAKE.   By G. H. STUART, M.A. 2s. 6d. ; sewed, 2s.   Canto I., sewed, 9d.

—THE LAY OF THE LAST MINSTREL.   By G. H. STUART, M.A., and E. H. ELLIOT, B.A.   2s.   Canto I., sewed, 9d.   Cantos I.-III., and IV.-VI., 1s. 3d. each; sewed, 1s. each.
The *Journal of Education*—"The text is well printed, and the notes, wherever we have tested them, have proved at once scholarly and simple."

MACMILLAN AND CO., LONDON.

SCOTT—MARMION. By MICHAEL MACMILLAN, B.A. 3s.; sewed, 2s. 6d.

The *Spectator*—" . . . His introduction is admirable, alike for point and brevity."

The *Indian Daily News*—"The present volume contains the poem in 200 pages, with more than 100 pages of notes, which seem to meet every possible difficulty."

—ROKEBY. By the same. 3s.; sewed, 2s. 6d.

The *Guardian*—"The introduction is excellent, and the notes show much care and research."

SHAKESPEARE—THE TEMPEST. By K. DEIGHTON. 1s. 9d.

The *Guardian*—" Speaking generally of Macmillan's Series we may say that they approach more nearly than any other edition we know to the ideal school Shakespeare. The introductory remarks are not too much burdened with controversial matter; the notes are abundant and to the point, scarcely any difficulty being passed over without some explanation, either by a paraphrase or by etymological and grammatical notes."

The *School Guardian*—"A handy edition of *The Tempest*, suitable for the use of colleges and schools generally. Mr. Deighton has prefixed to the volume an introduction on the date, origin, construction, and characters of the play, and has added a pretty full collection of notes, with an index of reference to the passages of the text in question. The 'get up' of this series is a model of what such books should be."

—MUCH ADO ABOUT NOTHING. By the same. 2s.
The *Schoolmaster*—" The notes on words and phrases are full and clear."

—A MIDSUMMER NIGHT'S DREAM. By the same. 1s. 9d.

—THE MERCHANT OF VENICE. By the same. 1s. 9d.

—AS YOU LIKE IT. By the same. 1s. 9d.

—TWELFTH NIGHT. By the same. 1s. 9d.
The *Educational News*—"This is an excellent edition of a good play."

—THE WINTER'S TALE. By the same. 2s.
The *Literary World*—"The Introduction gives a good historical and critical account of the play, and the notes are abundantly full."

—KING JOHN. By the same. 1s. 9d.

—RICHARD II. By the same. 1s. 9d.

—HENRY IV., Part I. By the same. 2s. 6d.; sewed, 2s.

—HENRY IV., Part II. By the same. 2s. 6d.; sewed, 2s.

—HENRY V. By the same. 1s. 9d.

—RICHARD III. By C. H. TAWNEY, M.A. 2s. 6d.; sewed, 2s.
The *School Guardian*—" Of Mr. Tawney's work as an annotator we can speak in terms of commendation. His notes are full and always to the point."

—HENRY VIII. By K. DEIGHTON. 1s. 9d.

—CORIOLANUS. By the same. 2s. 6d.; sewed, 2s.

—ROMEO AND JULIET. By the same. 2s. 6d.; sewed, 2s.

—JULIUS CAESAR. By the same. 1s. 9d.

—HAMLET. By K. DEIGHTON. 2s. 6d.; sewed, 2s.

MACMILLAN AND CO., LONDON.

SHAKESPEARE—MACBETH. By the same. 1s. 9d.
The *Educational Review*—"This is an excellent edition for the student. The notes are suggestive, . . . and the vivid character sketches of Macbeth and Lady Macbeth are excellent."

—KING LEAR. By the same. 1s. 9d.

—OTHELLO. By the same. 2s.

—ANTONY AND CLEOPATRA. By the same. 2s. 6d. ; sewed, 2s.

—CYMBELINE. By the same. 2s. 6d.; sewed, 2s.
The *Scotsman*—"Mr. Deighton has adapted his commentary, both in *Othello* and in *Cymbeline*, with great skill to the requirements and capacities of the readers to whom the series is addressed."

SOUTHEY—LIFE OF NELSON. By MICHAEL MACMILLAN, B.A.
   3s.; sewed, 2s. 6d.

SPENSER—THE FAERIE QUEENE. Book I. By H. M. PERCIVAL,
   M.A. 3s. ; sewed, 2s. 6d.

—SHEPHEARDS CALENDER. By Prof. C. H. HERFORD.

TENNYSON—SELECTIONS. By F. J. ROWE, M.A., and W. T.
   WEBB, M.A. 3s. 6d. Also in two Parts, 2s. 6d. each.
   Part I. Recollections of the Arabian Nights, The Lady of
   Shalott, The Lotos-Eaters, Dora, Ulysses, Tithonus, The
   Lord of Burleigh, The Brook, Ode on the Death of the
   Duke of Wellington, The Revenge.—Part II. Oenone, The
   Palace of Art, A Dream of Fair Women, Morte d'Arthur,
   Sir Galahad, The Voyage, and Demeter and Persephone.
The *Journal of Education*—"It should find a wide circulation in English schools. . . . . The notes give just the requisite amount of help for understanding Tennyson, explanations of the allusions with which his poems teem, and illustrations by means of parallel passages. A short critical introduction gives the salient features of his style with apt examples."
The *Literary World*—"The book is very complete, and will be a good introduction to the study of Tennyson's works generally."

—MORTE D'ARTHUR. By the same. 1s. sewed.

—ENOCH ARDEN. By W. T. WEBB, M.A. 2s. 6d.

—AYLMER'S FIELD. By W. T. WEBB, M.A. 2s. 6d.

—THE PRINCESS. By P. M. WALLACE, M.A. 3s. 6d.

—THE COMING OF ARTHUR ; THE PASSING OF ARTHUR. By
   F. J. ROWE, M.A. 2s. 6d.

—GARETH AND LYNETTE. By G. C. MACAULAY, M.A. 2s. 6d.

—THE MARRIAGE OF GERAINT ; GERAINT AND ENID. By G. C.
   MACAULAY, M.A. 2s. 6d.

—LANCELOT AND ELAINE. By F. J. ROWE, M.A. 2s. 6d.

—THE HOLY GRAIL. By G. C. MACAULAY, M.A. 2s. 6d.

—GUINEVERE. By G. C. MACAULAY, M.A.   [*In the Press.*

WORDSWORTH—SELECTIONS. By F. J. ROWE, M.A., and W. T.
   WEBB, M.A.   [*In preparation.*

MACMILLAN AND CO., LONDON.

20.5.95.

www.ingramcontent.com/pod-product-compliance
Lightning Source LLC
Chambersburg PA
CBHW032155010726
47493CB00008BA/2705